The Roaring Twenties Trilogy

Charleston's Lonely Heart Hotel
Charleston's House of Stuart
Charleston on the Potomac

The Belle Family Saga

The Pirate and the Belle
The Belles of Charleston
The Old Maids' Club
Charleston's Lonely Heart Hotel
Charleston's House of Stuart
Carolina Girls

Other books by Steve Brown

Black Fire
Radio Secrets
Hurricane Party
The Charleston Ripper
The Charleston Vampire

Charleston's House of Stuart

Charleston's House of Stuart

Steve Brown

CHICK SPRINGS
PUBLISHING™
SOUTH CAROLINA

First published in the USA in 2012 by
Chick Springs Publishing
PO Box 1130, Taylors, SC 29687
E-mail: ChickSprgs@aol.com
Web Site: www.chicksprings.com

Library of Congress Control Number: 2012911239
Library of Congress Data Available

ISBN: 978-0-9839824-1-8

10   9   8   7   6   5   4   3   2   1

Author's Note

Acknowledgments

For their assistance in preparing this story, I would like to thank Mark Brown, Sharon Gilstrap, Sally Heineman, Missy Johnson, Stacey King, Kate Lehman, Celia Miles, Stacey Randall, Susan Snowden, Helen Turnage, Ellis Vidler, Dwight Watt, and, of course, Mary Ella.

For Dashiell Hammett
Author of *The Thin Man*

The House of Stuart:

James Stuart	Head of the house
Hartleigh Stuart	His wife
Sue Ellen Hall	His sister
Jeb Stuart	His older brother
Tessa Stuart	His niece
Cousin Jimmy	From Greenville
Katie Stuart	Jimmy's wife
Jebbie Stuart	Katie's son
Eileen Stuart	James's mother
Alexander	Manservant
Pearl	His wife
Molly	Pearl's sister

The Belles of Charleston:

Franklin Belle, Senior	Father
Georgiana Belle	Stepmother
Franklin, Junior	Their bachelor son
Lewis Belle	The Stuarts' attorney
Rachel Belle	Married Christian Andersen
Christian Andersen	From Dairyland, Wisconsin
Luke Andersen	Christian's younger brother

Others:

Nell Ingram	Girl down the street
Billy Ray Craven	Assistant solicitor
Vincenzo Petrocelli	Bootlegger
Eddie Elliott	Speakeasy owner
Prescott Mitchell	Office manager
Polly Mitchell	His wife
Eugene Roddey	Warehouse manager

"I know of nothing fundamentally wrong
with the stock market or with the underlying
business and credit structure."

> Charles E. Mitchell
> Chairman
> National City Bank of New York
> October 22, 1929

PROLOGUE

Less than a month after the opening of the first bridge over the Cooper River (August 8, 1929), the Great Bull Market of the Roaring Twenties stumbled, and investors, seeing this as a chance to snap up some really cheap stocks, pushed stock prices back up. The following month the sell-off was so rapid that stock tickers could not keep up with the trading. This time bankers pooled their resources to prop up prices and halt the decline. Still, it was over three hours before the tickers finally caught up, and during this time brokers made phone calls and sent telegrams requesting that clients cover their margins. Most could not, and two days later, even though John D. Rockefeller stepped in and bought a sizable number of shares, nothing could stop the rout. By mid-November, thirty billion dollars' worth of stock value had vanished, and people immediately cut back on their spending, throwing millions of people out of work. This period in American history is known as the Panic of 1929.

ONE

Hartleigh was negotiating her household allowance with her husband when her father-in-law was found floating facedown in the Ashley River in the same general area where her new husband moored his yacht.

"James?"

Whatever he focused on, James Stuart's concentration was absolute. His nose remained firmly planted in the *News & Courier.*

The young couple had just finished dinner and were enjoying a cup of coffee in the parlor, James still in his three-piece suit, Hartleigh in maternity clothing. She was beginning her ninth month, that period of a pregnancy when you just want to put down the baby and walk away for a while.

"James!"

Her husband lowered the paper and looked at her. James Stuart was a tall, slender fellow with ropey muscles and a dark complexion from all the time he spent racing his yacht. His wife considered him to be the swellest of guys, but only if you could hold his attention.

A table and lamp sat between the couple, and behind their matching Queen Anne chairs, a small dry bar that folded away. Directly across from them stood the fireplace; flanking their right, a love seat, and between the two windows hung an old pier glass.

Hartleigh held out the list, giving the small sheet a little wave. When she did, the baby kicked.

James was taking the list when she gasped. He dropped his newspaper into his lap. "Are you all right?"

The larger this baby became, thought Hartleigh, the more difficult it became to take a deep breath. And whenever she left the house, Hartleigh always knew the location of the nearest public toilet, though she rarely went out, no more than a little strolling along the Battery. She'd cut way back on their social engagements. Still, she attended church three times a week, but absolutely no sailing!

"No, no, nothing. The baby just kicked."

James folded the newspaper and shoved it into the magazine rack beside his chair. The list of expenses he placed on the table. "Should I call the doctor?"

"James, the baby kicks all the time." His wife had that rosy countenance of a woman in the latter stage of pregnancy. She patted her tummy. "Perhaps he'll play football for the Citadel."

"More likely West Point." James had graduated from West Point as a civil engineer and he had previously been the site engineer for the first bridge built across the Cooper River.

Hartleigh rubbed her tummy again. "And how would I explain that to all our friends?"

"West Point is a national power in football, not the Citadel."

Hartleigh almost laughed. "James, have you ever considered that this baby might be a girl?"

At this her husband appeared genuinely puzzled, so Hartleigh picked up the list and handed it to him. James had promised more money for the church's soup kitchen if Hartleigh could rein in her expenses. And she must do something. Even those living south of Broad were showing up at the soup kitchen; others had gone north of Broad where no one would recognize them.

James looked up from the list. "Can this be right?"

"I can justify every single expense. Which item do you question?"

A slender young woman who favored James with her brown hair, narrow face, and lanky frame strolled into the parlor. She wore the distinctive flapper garb: short dress with the waistline dropped to the hip and a hemline just below the knee; if the wind hit it, the hem was sure to reveal a garter belt holding up a pair of rayon stockings. Sue Ellen's hair, which had once been bobbed, was now cut even shorter, into a "shingle," or a slicked-down cut with a curl on each side covering her ears. A felt, bell-shaped hat and Mary Jane shoes completed her outfit.

"Billy Ray's on his way. We're going to Sullivan's Island."

"That's not appropriate. You're a married woman."

"And no longer pregnant."

Sue Ellen had lost her baby, and most of her friends believed the loss was due to her attending all those Christmas parties. Tongues always wagged about Sue Ellen, mainly because she and her husband didn't live together. Actually, anyone who deviated from the norm was fair game south of Broad, and Sue Ellen was definitely a grass widow.

"Don't wait up."

"Sue Ellen, you're not to do this." James glanced at his wife, but found Hartleigh judiciously examining the list of household expenses. "You're getting a reputation."

"No matter what you say, I'm not moving to New York."

"You should've considered that before you married a civil engineer. Engineers go where the jobs are."

"Easy for you to say, brother dear, you made a killing in the stock market and don't have to work."

"We're not discussing this. You are not to leave this house unless it's to rejoin your husband in New York. Molly will help you pack." Molly was the household maid.

Hartleigh rose from her chair.

"Please don't," said Sue Ellen, extending her arm toward Hartleigh. "I'll be the one leaving."

But Hartleigh had heard a knock at the front door. Now that knock came again.

"That'll be Billy Ray," said Sue Ellen, heading out of the parlor. Billy Ray never used the bell, only knocked.

Hartleigh eased back down into her chair and James rose to his feet.

His voice followed Sue Ellen out of the parlor. "You were once engaged to Billy Ray. What will people think?"

"James," whispered his wife, "let her go."

He sat back down. "But I'm responsible for her."

"Indeed you are, but sooner or later you must give your sister her head."

"She knows I can't send her home." Sue Ellen could not live at home as their father became rather mean-spirited when he drank, and nowadays he stayed tight all the time. "It's just not fair."

"Girls don't play fair, darling. We play to win."

Sue Ellen returned to the parlor with a heavyset, red-headed man. Billy Ray and James had attended Charleston's Male High School together. Tonight, Billy Ray did not speak to James, nor offer to shake hands. A growing tension had developed between the two men as rumors swirled around the amount of time Sue Ellen spent dancing on Sullivan's Island.

"Billy Ray's here to see you, James."

Billy Ray held his derby in his hands instead of hanging it on the hat rack in the hall. He directed his remarks to the pregnant woman.

"Evening, Hartleigh."

"Good evening, Billy Ray."

"Hope you're doing well."

"So very nice of you to ask."

He glanced at her abdomen. "Well, I hope it's a boy."

"So does James."

"If you have business with me," said James, rising, "why didn't you call and make an appointment?"

The chief of police followed Billy Ray into the parlor. A burly, garrulous man, he said, "Captain Stuart, long time, no see." To Hartleigh, "Nice to see you again, Mrs. Stuart."

That was a reference to Hartleigh showing up at the city jail to plead for her boyfriend's release last year. It was the same night James had proposed marriage and Hartleigh had eagerly accepted.

The chief nodded to Sue Ellen. "Mrs. Hall." He, too, held his derby in his hands.

James headed out of the parlor and down the hall. "The study is this way."

"We're not going dancing?" asked Sue Ellen.

"Not tonight, honey. I have business to attend to."

The chief of police followed James into the hall and gestured at the front door. "If you don't mind, Captain Stuart, could we speak outside?"

Normally, James would have insisted on speaking in his study, with a closed door between these men and others in the house. His sister, however, had embarrassed him, putting him off his stride. He agreed to talk with the men on the front porch.

With a last look at the furniture, the mirrors, and the family portraits lining the walls, the chief followed James and Billy Ray outside, closing the door behind him.

The porch was a wraparound on a three-story house and overlooked a postage-stamp front yard, South Battery, Murray Boulevard, and finally, the rock seawall buttressing White Point Gardens.

A breeze blew across the Ashley, rattling the fronds of the palmettos. Billy Ray's Model A sports coupe was parked at the curb, as was a patrol car with the beat cop leaning against the hood and smoking a cigarette. At the appearance of the chief, the beat cop rolled off the car and flicked away his cigarette.

The chief asked, "Is it true your ancestor—the original James Stuart—killed Blackbeard?"

James glanced at Billy Ray. "I hardly think you

came here tonight for a history lesson, Chief."

"It's true," said Billy Ray, nodding to the chief.

"How the mighty have fallen. Your father was once an important figure in Charleston."

James leveled his gaze at the chief. "Is there a point to this conversation?"

Billy Ray glanced at the Ashley. "Kind of breezy out here, Chief. Maybe we should get to the point."

"Captain Stuart, your father is one of the biggest bootleggers in this city."

"And I'm a civil engineer."

"Well, in the future that may change—"

"Is that what you came by for, to warn me not to become a bootlegger?"

Billy Ray watched this exchange with considerable anxiety. The Stuarts were not to be toyed with, even if you had the law on your side.

"James," said Billy Ray, "a patrolman found some-one floating in the Ashley near the marina. It appears to be your father."

Inside the house, Sue Ellen continued to fume. "I'm twenty-five years old and I'm being treated like a child. It's nineteen-thirty—a new decade, a new century—and I should be able to go wherever I please."

"But those passing judgment on you were born in the previous century," argued Hartleigh, "and they're still rather old-fashioned about what a married woman can do and what she cannot."

"Cousin Katie does anything she cares to—flies a plane, reports for a newspaper."

"Katie Stuart lives in the upstate, not south of Broad."

Sue Ellen scuffed one of her Mary Jane shoes at the circular rug. "You seem to be taking my brother's side a lot these days." This was Sue Ellen at her most disingenuous as she had engineered Hartleigh and James's courtship right up to their marriage.

Peeking from under her cloche hat, Sue Ellen asked, "Are you choosing him over me?"

Hartleigh laughed, then straightened up, making her abdomen more prominent. "Not after what your brother did to me."

Sue Ellen took a seat in her brother's chair, brushed down the hem of her dress, and picked up the list of household expenditures.

She quickly read through it. "You really think you can stick to this?"

"James says we must economize."

"Daddy says the economy will snap back. It always has."

"I don't know. James thinks this will be much worse than in the past. A good many people now live in the city and they have nowhere to go."

Sue Ellen put down the list and picked at her hemline. Like many young women, Sue Ellen kept a diary, and she could not believe the number of times the word "depression" had crept into the text. "I wish you'd take that money Edmund sends each month. The part that should go toward your household expenses I spend on King Street."

"You can stay as long as you like. You're not only family but my best friend."

Sue Ellen got up and began to pace from the Queen Anne chairs to the fireplace and back again. The fringe on her dress swayed.

She stopped and studied the fire. "Perhaps I should move to New York, but leaving Charleston . . . I just couldn't do that. Charleston is my home."

Hartleigh simply listened. Without her brother around, Sue Ellen was not all that cocksure.

She returned to her chair and plopped down. Again, she brushed down the hemline of her short dress. "I don't know what's to become of me. Before I lost the baby, I knew what life held: a husband, children, my own household. Now what? There's no way I'll get pregnant with Edmund in New York." Sue Ellen hoped Hartleigh would never learn the terrible secret she had withheld from her best friend. Actually, she was having trouble coming to grips with it herself.

"This, too, will pass," said Hartleigh. "Besides, I'll need all the help I can get when the baby arrives."

"Me take the baby away from Pearl? She'll never allow it." Pearl and her younger sister, Molly, were the cook and the maid who lived in the carriage house; and all the two Negroes talked about was the arrival of the new baby.

"I'd have a better chance with Rachel. She's carrying twins." Sue Ellen sat up. "I can't believe Rachel hasn't returned home to have her babies."

"I'm sure there are plenty of capable doctors in Wisconsin."

Rachel Andersen, née Belle, had gone north for an extended visit and remained in Wisconsin with her husband's family. Any farm could always use an extra hand, though neither Sue Ellen nor Hartleigh could envision a Belle of Charleston performing menial chores. Rachel Belle had never done a day's work in her life.

Sue Ellen shivered. "It's so cold up there. There's always snow on the ground whenever she writes."

"I'm confident that Rachel has adapted. She's a strong-willed young woman."

"But for generations Belle children have been born in Charleston—even women who moved away always came home to give birth."

"You're about to be an aunt. Can't you occupy your time spoiling your nephew or niece until you have one of your own?"

Sue Ellen got to her feet and began to pace again. After a turn back and forth, she said, "I get up each morning and once I've finished my toilet and had a cup of coffee, I sit there wondering what I'm going to do for the day. There are just so many garden parties a girl can attend or games of mahjong she can play."

"Have you considered working in a soup kitchen?"

"Me in a kitchen?" She laughed. "That would be a disaster." She stopped her pacing and faced Hartleigh. "I thought this was the proper way to live your life."

"Pardon?"

"Get married. Start a family."

"It is. Every woman should have a family. It's what being a woman is all about."

"But what if I can't have children? Then what am I to do with the rest of my life?"

TWO

In Dairyland, Wisconsin, Rachel Belle Andersen slipped on a wet kitchen floor and sat down hard.

"Oh!"

A wave of anger washed over her and she came close to taking the Lord's name in vain. Heading into the ninth month and carrying twins, Rachel found it impossible to return to her feet. She rolled over on one hip, then the other, but she could not get to her feet; even on her hands and knees she could not stand up.

She wanted to pound the floor and scream. Instead, she grabbed a chair, which fell over but didn't make enough noise to draw attention to her plight.

Rachel considered her predicament. What to do? Scream and holler? Or be found crying while sitting helplessly on the kitchen floor?

She had tried to make this marriage work, going so far as to follow her husband to Wisconsin where they were put to work saving the family farm. Nicholas Eaton, a young man who had had designs on her until Rachel became engaged to Christian, had written to her, suggesting that the couple come to New York where he and Edmund Hall, Sue Ellen's husband, were building the Empire State Building. They could get Christian on the staff before the foundation was poured, but they had to hurry.

And why shouldn't they move? It appeared she'd married into a family that promoted raising milk prices by barricading roads, stopping trucks, and pouring milk onto the side of the road. For some odd reason, farmers who produced milk for bottling were prospering, but those producing milk for cheese and butter, like the Andersens, were facing foreclosure. And facing the loss of the family farm, and a county deeply polarized by the milk/cheese issue, the Andersens had taken to carrying shotguns or rifles wherever they went.

Several months ago, two young men had set upon Christian while he was loading groceries into the backseat of the car. The trip to town had been a way for Rachel to get out of the house for a few hours, but it was the last time she ever went into town.

When Christian ignored the hecklers, one of them locked his hands together and thumped her husband across the back of his shoulders. Christian went to his knees and the groceries he carried fell across the backseat and tumbled to the floorboard. The two thugs began pummeling him when he tried to return to his feet.

Rachel screamed, but no one came. Many stopped and stared. Before she knew it, Rachel was out of the car, dragging the shotgun off the dashboard and across her seat. When the shotgun thumped off the passenger seat and hit the ground, Rachel realized she'd have to use both hands to bring up the double-barrel; in the air, once again, she found she could not control the long gun.

The double-barrel fell to the hood of the car, and as Rachel tried to steady the weapon, her finger accidentally pulled one of the triggers. A barrel discharged, Rachel screamed, and the shotgun slipped from her hands. When she looked again, the two toughs were running down the street, and the shotgun lay beside the car.

Rachel helped her husband back to his feet and into the car. By then, a small crowd had gathered, and one of the men passed the shotgun through the window after assisting Rachel into the car and closing the door behind her.

"You need the police?" he asked across Rachel.

"No, no," said Christian, waving off the suggestion as he hunched forward at the wheel, trying to catch his breath.

Another man stepped to Christian's side of the car and closed the door for him. "It's just starting, Christian, and you can expect more of the same. Your family's on the wrong side of this issue."

Christian saw his wife taking the shotgun through the window from the man who had helped her into the car. He grabbed the double barrel and lifted it up and out of his face. Reversing the weapon, he broke the action and removed the shells.

"Thank you," said Christian to the fellow on Rachel's side of the car. He cranked the engine, put the car into gear, and drove out of town. And it took a lot less time to return to the farm than it had to drive into town.

A young blonde entered the kitchen, saw Rachel sitting in the middle of the floor, and rushed to her side. "Rachel, what happened?"

"I'm . . . I'm sorry." Rachel's white skin flushed. "I slipped."

The blonde tried to assist the raven-haired girl to her feet. It was no use. Rachel was far too heavy.

"Wait right here. I'll get some help."

"Thank you, Lene." Rachel fought back the tears. This was so humiliating, and even more so when Lene returned with Rachel's mother-in-law. By the time they had her on her feet and into a chair, Rachel had decided that she would pack her bags and leave that very night.

"Here," said her sister-in-law, offering a glass of milk. "If we can't make cheese, we can at least drink it."

Rachel thanked her and sipped from the glass. She had earned a grudging respect from the women of this house because of her hard work and good nature. Everyone in Wisconsin seemed to have seen *Birth of a Nation* and thought Rachel would be your typical southern belle who expected to be waited on hand and foot.

Rachel had surprised them all by appearing in the kitchen her very first morning in Dairyland, and well before any of the men were up. And it was her clothing as much as her demeanor: altered hand-me-downs with sleeves covering her arms and a hem falling to her ankles. She abandoned her corset before the men returned for lunch. You had to be able to move around if you intended to work on a farm.

In the beginning, she had been given the nastiest of chores, such as washing up after meals or cleaning the only bathroom in the house, not to mention milking cows. But as Rachel began to show, her sister-in-law, Lene, made sure Rachel always had someone by her side to lift heavy objects or simply pick up things, which would now appear to include Rachel herself.

Not only did Rachel not complain, she never let on that as the date of her delivery approached, she was terrified of giving birth in the backwoods of Wisconsin, let alone twins. Only when she was occasionally left alone with the cows did Rachel have a good cry.

Rachel finished her milk, washed her glass, and left it in the wooden dish drainer. In the hallway she picked up the telephone and asked the operator to place a long distance call.

"Oh, Rachel. How are you?"

Rachel was always put off by the number of people who recognized her, even if they hadn't met her. In the Midwest, the voice of a Southerner definitely stood out. At church or a dance, people would say: "Oh, please don't stop talking" or "We just love to hear you talk." Another sore point: in Charleston, she would be addressed as "Miss Belle" or "Mrs. Andersen," never "Rachel."

"Er . . . fine, just fine. Could you place a call for me, please?"

Rachel gave the operator the number, and because she had never placed a long distance call before—they were terribly expensive—the operator assumed the number was Rachel's home in Charleston.

And she played along. "Please ask for Hartleigh. She's my sister-in-law." Rachel chuckled. "My mother has a phobia about talking on the phone, and the rest of the family will talk my ear off, so please reverse the charges and ask for Hartleigh."

"Certainly, Rachel. I'll get right back to you, and you take care of those babies."

When her husband came in for dinner, Rachel could present him, as well as the other members of the family, with a fait accompli. The Andersens had four sons; three were married and all three couples lived in the farmhouse, causing Lene, the old maid of the family, to bunk with her mother and her father. Seventeen-year-old Luke slept on a sofa in the family room with an assortment of nieces and nephews, who slept on pallets. Rachel and Christian shared a room with a married brother and his wife, a blanket hanging from the ceiling to provide some degree of privacy. The fourth couple lived on a small porch converted into a bedroom. As it was the farthest from the Franklin stove, it was the coldest room in the house. Old newspapers stuffed in cracks kept the temperature from falling below freezing.

Rachel flashed a cheery smile at those sitting around the table. "I'd rather deliver at home. Not that I won't miss y'all, but you must understand."

That was explanation enough for the women, but her father-in-law asked, "When do you leave?"

Everyone looked at Christian.

"Oh, no!" said Rachel. "I'm not about to drag Christian away from spring planting. As the daughter of a plantation owner, I know how important spring planting is."

After supper, Christian loaded the car while his mother put together a picnic basket. "You'll travel alone?" she asked Rachel.

"The train out of Duluth has a sleeper, and th members of the Brotherhood of Sleeping Car Porters are quite used to southern ladies traveling alone. Most of the porters were born below the Mason-Dixon Line." Rachel turned to Christian. "Didn't you find that to be so, darling, when we traveled north?"

Christian nodded that he had.

Still, the family believed this girl from Dixie was putting a great deal of faith in members of a race that no one but Christian had ever seen. So Christian was detailed to accompany his wife on her return to Charleston; Luke went along to return the car from Duluth.

"Just who's paying for all these long distance phone calls?" asked her father-in-law.

His wife shot him an angry look while Rachel explained that she had reversed the charges on the call to Charleston. From a small purse, she counted out the exact charge for the call made to Duluth to locate the sleeping car.

"Put your money away, Rachel," said her mother-in-law as she wrapped the sandwiches in wax paper. "You're a member of this family, too."

Later in the car, an aging, four-door Oldsmobile touring car used to attend church and to haul supplies from town, Christian grinned wickedly. "Will this be a second honeymoon?"

Rachel had been checking the backseat where her suitcase and genuine leather overnight bag sat on top of a Jenny Lind trunk. Sitting beside the Jenny Lind and holding Rachel's shoe bag was Luke Andersen. Though seventeen years old, Luke had rarely been off the family farm, so traveling to Duluth made the young man's eyes shine with excitement.

CHARLESTON'S HOUSE OF STUART

The leather shoe bag summed up Rachel's stay north of the Mason-Dixon Line. Inside was room for eight pairs of shoes, of which Rachel had worn only three; her tango shoes, destroyed by the mud and snow of Wisconsin, had been thrown away after one barn dance. Rachel immediately wired Sears, Roebuck for two pairs of sensibly laced shoes with round toes and lower wedge heels. Those shoes and a pair of boots with fleece lining had been left behind for Lene.

Rachel took Christian's arm. "No, sirree, my dear. Last time you traveled with a carefree bride, but this trip you're traveling with a pregnant fishwife."

Christian smiled warmly. "At least I'll be with you."

Approaching the county line, they saw a pickup straddling the road. Christian brought the Olds to a stop and two men armed with a shotgun and a squirrel rifle appeared out of the darkness.

THREE

The Belles of Charleston sat at the dinner table as they always did: Franklin, Senior; his second wife, Georgiana; and Franklin, Junior. Franklin, Junior, represented the eleventh generation of Belles in the New World and was a member of one of the most prominent families south of Broad. The Belles lived in a grand house overlooking the Ashley, all because of some serious sacrifices made by Catherine Belle over two hundred years ago when she and her sister escaped the Parisian mobs by taking the underground railroad to Switzerland and onto London where they sailed for Charles Towne. Also in the dining room stood two servants as silent and unnoticed as the furniture.

Georgiana cleared her throat, and the two men looked at her end of the table. Franklin, Senior, and his wife sat at opposite ends of a table that would seat twenty, though pulled up to today's table were only four chairs. A single chair sat opposite son Franklin, but whether the empty chair was there as a reminder of the missing Rachel or a chair for Franklin's nonexistent wife, neither father nor son knew, nor did they dare ask. They were about to find out.

"When Rachel returns, she will call the following Sunday."

Her husband stared down the table. "And why would I care to know this, my dear?"

"So you can lunch at your club once you've dropped Franklin and me off after church."

"Very considerate of you, Georgiana."

"I will expect you to be at that meal, Franklin."

"Of course, Mother."

"That is, if you have no other plans."

"I do not."

There was a long pause, then: "You're in excellent health, my son?"

Franklin finished chewing a piece of his Atlantic black grouper. He swallowed before saying, "I'm not sure I understand the question."

"Any questions directed to a young gentleman over the age of thirty will always be concerned with his marital prospects."

Franklin sighed and put down his fork.

"A young woman should be sitting across from you, either as your fiancée or your bride, or better yet, as the mother of your children."

Franklin tried to speak, but his stepmother raised her hand. "If an available young woman sat across from you every Sunday, I might be able to embarrass you into providing this family with an heir, which is your sole responsibility."

"Since there are so many men out of work, one would think that my most important responsibility would be to hold down a job."

"No. That's your responsibility to your wife and children."

Franklin scooted his chair backward and took his napkin from his lap. He stood up and dropped the napkin on the table.

"Now, dear, don't be rude."

"I hardly think I'm the one being rude." He looked at his father. "May I be excused?"

His father gestured at the other end of the table. "This is your mother's table, not mine."

Franklin's face darkened as he faced Georgiana. "Madam, may I be excused?"

"Of course, my dear, but be forewarned that the place across from you will have a young woman sitting there every Sunday from now on, and you are expected to be in attendance."

"Then, perhaps I will join my father at his club."

"If I must embarrass you into marriage, I'm perfectly willing to do so."

"So I see."

"Franklin!" said his father, raising his voice. "Don't be rude to your mother."

"Stepmother."

Senior put down his fork. "Apologize, boy, or I'll find my buggy whip and wear it out on you!"

Without looking in her direction, her stepson apologized.

"You have an obligation to produce an heir," continued Georgiana, "and I don't mean some yard child, but the next heir of this great house. Otherwise, you'll find yourself on the street."

"Or living at Cooper Hill."

"If your cousin's wife allows it. Her husband is next in line to inherit both this house and Cooper Hill.

You know the terms of the will: oldest son inherits unless he has no male heir. The Belle house on the Battery is to be filled with families, not bachelors or old maids. It's well known that other members of the family covet this house. Not so long ago your father's family moved in when your great uncle moved north, and if you don't commit to some young woman, vultures will soon be circling our home and measuring its windows for new trimmings."

"We've had this conversation before, Mother."

"But not when everyone in Charleston knew Rachel was expecting."

"Georgiana," said her husband at the other end of the table, "I asked that that name never again be mentioned in my presence."

"Yes, my darling, but Franklin's lackadaisical attitude endangers my future, too. You are sure to predecease me. Am I destined to live in some state of legal limbo until that uncertain state brings an end to my life?"

"You don't know that, my dear."

"Please. If I'm to be cut off from my grandchildren because of the disinheritance of our only daughter, then it's every member of this family for themselves."

At the other end of the table, Senior let out a long sigh. He looked at his son. "Find a bride, Franklin, the sooner, the better."

"But, Father—"

"Sorry, but your ride on the gravy train ends today."

"Sir," said his wife, "I find your use of slang at this table offensive."

"Then I apologize." To his son: "Marry, my boy."

"Father, I grew up south of Broad and none of these girls interest me."

"Then get invited to Savannah or Augusta and find your bride there. We certainly know people in both towns."

"Augusta, Georgia?"

"Yes. Who knows who you'll meet."

"A woman who plays golf most likely."

"Franklin, my dear," said his stepmother, "women of your generation have been doing all sorts of trivial things with their lives. I would've thought you'd be accustomed to it by now."

"Really, Mother, a golfer?"

"Find a bride," said his father, "and leave us in peace."

"And she doesn't have to have a significant dowry."

Franklin gave Georgiana a modified bow, bringing his heels together, head down, and hands clinching into fists. "By your leave, madam."

Once the young man had left the room, Georgiana said, "The boy's thirty-two and has no prospects."

Her husband said nothing.

"There's talk," added Georgiana.

Senior glanced at the servants.

Georgiana called the two black people by name and asked them for a moment. The servants disappeared into the kitchen, closing the door behind them.

From his end of the table, her husband asked, "Am I to take the boy to a bordello to see if his equipment works properly?"

"Franklin, my dear, you've been quite vulgar enough for one meal." Georgiana cleared her throat. "His best friend assures me there's nothing wrong with our son."

Her husband could not believe what he was hearing. "You actually inquired as to our son's interest in the opposite sex?"

"Rachel is pregnant. That changes everything."

"And I asked you not to say her name in my presence."

"You can have your way with this, my darling, but not to the point where it embarrasses the family."

Franklin was always astonished at how much more ardent those who married into the family were at honoring its traditions than those who had been born into it.

"You are quite aware that your daughter is a natural born leader and can easily mobilize her generation against us."

Senior shook his head. "I wish Franklin had her nerve."

"Then it's settled. I will oversee the engagement of our son to a suitable young lady who shall become my spy in Rachel's camp."

"Come again?"

"Do you really believe you can win this struggle without my support? At any moment, Hartleigh's mother could return from her Grand Tour, and I will not allow our grandchildren to be subject to all that drama."

"The grandchildren are dead to me, too."

She continued as if not hearing him. "And if there is any slipup by Rachel or her husband, I shall be there to scoop up their babies."

FOUR

In the light of the Oldsmobile's headlights, Rachel could see a third man—a kid—standing in the bed of the pickup. In the boy's hands appeared to be a .22-caliber rifle. From the backseat, Luke leaned forward for a better look.

Christian rolled down his window. On her side, Rachel raised a gloved hand to shield her eyes from the beam of a flashlight. Her left hand remained inside her muff.

"Well, well, and who do we have here?" asked the man at the rolled-down window. He rested a foot on the running board, then looked at Rachel and tipped his slouch hat. "Ma'am."

The man on Rachel's side of the Olds worked his light around the interior. "Just what's going on here?" His light stopped on Luke, who stared at his feet. "Don't I know you, boy?"

Luke gulped and looked away.

"Roll down the window, Mrs. Andersen."

Rachel did as asked.

When Christian's hands came off the wheel, the man on his side of the car raised his shotgun. "If you know what's good for you, you'll keep your hands on that wheel."

Christian's hands returned to the wheel. "What do you want, Kasper?"

"One of your neighbors noticed all the activity at your house and called ahead." He flashed his light at Rachel. "You married the wrong man, Mrs. Andersen. In Wisconsin, milkmen rule, not cheeseheads. Now, out of the car! We're going to teach your husband a lesson or two."

Rachel leaned across her husband. "My family's not political, sir. Last time we tried that, it didn't work out, so these days we steer clear of politics."

"Kasper," asked Christian, "are you telling me you have people watching our house?"

Kasper ignored the question. "Remember last year when your brothers dragged my cousin out of his truck and dumped his milk beside the road?"

"I wouldn't know anything about that. I was building a bridge in Charleston."

"Then you should've stayed down south." The man on Rachel's side of the car gestured at Luke with his squirrel rifle. "Out of the car, boy!"

Luke hastily stacked the shoe bag on top of the Jenny Lind and opened the rear door.

"Luke," said Rachel, "stay in the car."

The command was issued with such authority that Luke did not know what to do. Air rushed through the open back door and the rolled-down windows. It was cold, but that was not the reason Luke shivered.

"Don't buck me, boy," said the man on Rachel's side of the car. "You've been sparking my daughter, and on more than one occasion been told not to come around."

"Watch your tongue, sir, you're frightening the boy."

"Shut your mouth, lady. This is between the men-folk."

"No," said Rachel, "this is between your family and mine." And she pulled a derringer from her muff and shot the man in the chest. The man stumbled back, dropped the squirrel rifle, and clutched his chest. He eased himself down to the road.

Rachel turned the gun on Kasper. "Let us go, sir! I beg of you."

Instead, Kasper brought up his shotgun, so Rachel shot him, too. When her husband's response was to only gape at her, she said, "It's only a two-shot, honey, so we'd best leave right away." To the boy in the backseat: "Close the door, Luke."

But her terrified brother-in-law did not move until Christian drew a Colt Peacemaker from under his seat. On the other side of the car, Kasper appeared at the rolled-down window, one hand holding onto the car, the other clutching his chest.

He stared at Rachel. "You shot me, lady."

Christian gestured with the Peacemaker and Kasper backed off. Only then did Christian pull the pistol back into the car and stomp on the accelerator.

"Get down, honey. There's still one in the bed of the pickup."

Rachel lay her head in his lap, and in the backseat Luke put his head between his knees and prayed. As he drove past the pickup, Christian saw the boy aim his rifle at them.

Christian threw a couple of shots in the boy's direction, and it had the desired effect of keeping the boy's head down.

Rachel tried to sit up.

"No! Not yet."

There was the ping of a .22 round hitting the trunk of the car, but by then they were gone.

In the backseat, his brother sobbed.

"You all right, Luke?" called out Rachel.

"Yes . . . yes, ma'am."

"Good, because you're about to pay a visit to Charleston."

Less than ten minutes later, two more pickups pulled to a stop at the scene of the shooting. These two men had been part of the blocking party but had received word too late to participate. A hysterical boy—Kasper's son—waved them to a stop. They found Kasper and Magnus wounded but not seriously injured.

"What happened?"

The boy tried to explain, something about a bunch of men shooting at him from a speeding car. The wounded adults told a different story, both men sitting on opposite sides of the road and clutching their chests.

"What happened?" repeated one of the later arrivals. Taking a handkerchief from his pocket, he pressed it against Kasper's chest.

Kasper explained that he and Magnus had been ambushed by Christian's wife.

"You let a woman get the drop on you?" All of these men were familiar with cowboy lingo from any number of Tom Mix movies.

"She had . . . she had a derringer in her muff," said Magnus, who was on his feet and being helped across the road.

"A derringer?"

"No, no," screamed Kasper's son. "It was a bigger gun than any derringer! I know. They shot at me with it!"

It was another few minutes before they finally sorted things out; then they placed Kasper and Magnus, along with their weapons, in the bed of the pickup.

"You going to be all right, kid?"

The boy's hands shook until he gripped the wheel. He had trouble getting the pickup into gear.

The late arrivals watched the pickup drive away.

"Never make it to the doctor."

"Not our concern. They broke the rule. You're to outnumber anyone you stop, then there's little chance of gunplay."

The other man continued to stare down the road. "We should be able to catch them before they reach Duluth."

"To what good, Tobias? The whole point of this exercise was to make Christian Andersen reconsider his return to Dairyland. Looks to me like he's gone for good. I can't imagine him ever coming back to Wisconsin."

"Then we don't have to catch them?"

"That's the work of the state police, that is, if Kasper's willing to admit a woman got the drop on him."

"But someone has to avenge them."

"Do what you like." Heading for his pickup, he added, "I'm going home. If Kasper and Magnus want to even the score, they know where the Andersens are headed."

FIVE

Katie Stuart was a fraud, but a very successful one. Katie had been orphaned by a moonshine feud in the Carolina foothills and taken in by three old maids who were members of the Belle family in the upstate. Katie made the most of her opportunity and had become a respected reporter for the Greenville *Piedmont* and flew her own plane to chase down stories. The day following the death of Jeb Stuart, Senior, Katie's husband traveled south by train with their two younger sons while Katie flew east toward the tobacco fields of Florence County. Since there were few landing strips in South Carolina, Katie zeroed in on a dirt road.

"I believe that's the one!" she shouted into the speaking tube.

Her oldest son, Jebbie, had been flying with his mother since he was nine, as it would appear that Katie's husband couldn't say no to his wife. This particular model, the Stearnman C3, Katie's second aircraft, was a rugged biplane with two open cockpits, the forward one seating two passengers.

"What do you see?"

Using a pair of German binoculars, the boy pointed at the crowd assembled in front of a farmhouse. "Got to be the place!"

Parked along the road were mostly pickups but also a few sedans, and assembled in front of the house was a crowd of thirty or forty men and boys staring up at them from land that had once been part of a thousand acres of gently rolling farmland with excellent drainage. Through sales and inheritances the original thousand acres had been reduced to less than one hundred, and the earlier crops of corn, wheat, indigo, and cotton had finally given way to tobacco. The original log cabin had been replaced by a two-story wood frame house, then by a mansion that was burned to the ground by the Yankees. Only the old oak-lined driveway remained, still leading to the ruins and splitting the hundred-acre farm right down the middle.

"And the road?" asked his mother through the speaking tube.

"Nothing moving."

"Okay. I'm going in."

"Roger that."

The biplane swept around in an arc, waved its wings, and lined up with an east-west county road. Just before touchdown, a man ran off the shoulder and into the field after throwing a shovelful of dirt in a hole. There were several places on the road that had been filled in. People on the ground shaded their eyes and drifted toward the road as the biplane bumped to a landing.

When the plane stopped, Katie stood up, pulled off her helmet, and shook out her golden hair. The crowd, mostly men and boys, burst into cheers, then applauded as she took her son's hand and leaped to the ground. Katie left her helmet in her seat and unzipped her leather jacket. From inside the jacket, she pulled a steno pad and the stub of a pencil. The leather jacket she tossed into the cockpit while her son applied the chocks to the wheels.

Sticking the pencil behind her ear, Katie strode into the crowd. Everyone welcomed her with smiles and a few handshakes, the exceptions being the auctioneer, the representative from the bank, and the reporter from *The State*. Katie wore trousers, riding boots, and a very tight-fitting blouse.

A representative to the South Carolina House tossed away his shovel and extended a hand. "Mrs. Stuart, Gerald Halley." He smiled at Jebbie. "And who is this?"

Katie put a hand on her son's shoulder. "Jeb Stuart. My son and copilot. He flies everywhere with me."

There were low whistles from the men, and a few of their sons became wide-eyed at the thought of such adventures.

"You can fly the plane, son?" asked Halley.

"Ever since I was ten. Mother didn't learn to fly until she was sixteen."

Katie clapped him on the shoulder. "Watch your tone, boy, or I'll kiss you right here in front of all these men."

Jebbie pulled away.

Katie returned her attention to the politician. "Thank you for inviting us here today."

Halley glanced at the other reporter. "We need to keep *The State* on their toes."

"You could've stayed in Greenville," said Bob Bass. "I file with United Press every day." The reporter, a dumpy man, wore a plaid coat, white shirt, suspenders, and a red bow tie. There were sweat stains under his arms.

Katie took his arm and patted it. "Oh, Bobby, I don't mean to be a bother, but us girls have to stay out of the office; otherwise, we end up fetching coffee and donuts for the real reporters." Katie took the pencil stub from behind her ear and turned her attention to the representative from the South Carolina House. "What have we got here?"

"A simple foreclosure, lady," said the man from the bank, "and we'd like to get on with it. Just who the devil are you anyway?"

"Katie Stuart with the Greenville *Piedmont*."

"A girl reporter? I thought you were some daredevil pilot."

"Oh, I'm that too," said Katie, smiling.

The politician introduced him, "This is 'Hap' Walton of the Florence Building and Loan."

"Just make sure you get your facts straight," said Walton. "My bank has an extensive legal department."

"Don't worry. I have Bobby here to backstop me."

Walton shook his head before stalking back to the porch. "Girl reporters—what next?"

"Backstop you?" asked Bass.

"Oh, Bobby," said Katie, touching his arm again, "I grew up watching 'Shoeless Joe' play for the Greenville Spinners. I should know what a baseball backstop is."

Jebbie realized that these farmers' sons had less

interest in the foreclosure than his plane. He asked to be excused so he could make a few nickels off the ones who had the nerve to climb up and sit in the forward seat.

"Still up to your old tricks, are you?" asked Bass.

"Oh, Bobby," gushed Katie again, "you know us girls would be nowhere if not for men like you."

Bass snorted. "Sarcasm doesn't become you, Mrs. Stuart." Of the South Carolina representative, Bass asked, "Something you don't like about the coverage you're getting from *The State*?"

"We need Washington's attention." The politician gestured at the surrounding property. "This farm has been in the Lyttleton family since before the Revolutionary War. You can trace their lineage back to a governor who signed a treaty with the Cherokees."

"So," said Bass, "the Lyttletons took this land from the Indians and now it's being taken from them."

"Oh, Bobby, think of the children."

As Katie moved to where the bidding had already begun, she saw the Lyttletons huddled at the far end of the porch, their hands on the shoulders of four sullen children.

Bob Bass muttered, "*She's* the future of journalism?"

"She looks pretty good to me," said the house rep.

"Yeah, but that doesn't make her all that able."

Katie was surprised that the bids were rather minuscule, and those who purchased the furniture, implements, and land were already talking to the Lyttletons about buying them back. The mood of the crowd was, well, hopeful and serene.

"That's the picture, Mrs. Belle," said the politician, who had joined her at the foot of the porch. "The people of Florence County stick together."

"You bust your butt," said the high bidder. "Sorry for the language, Mrs. Stuart, but when a man works hard he should have something to show for it, something to leave his family."

The auctioneer stomped down the stairs past the sheriff, but Hap Walton stopped to have a word with the law.

"You need to stop this foolishness, Sheriff. This is the third auction they've disrupted in a week."

"What folks bid is none of my concern."

"Fifty dollars for a farm, a dollar for a tractor, and fifty cents for a living room full of furniture—you call that fair?"

"Times are tough, Walton," commented one of the bidders.

Katie hastily scribbled all this in her steno pad.

"You're not going to get away with this," said Walton, looking around at the bidders. "We know what you're up to."

Several of the bidders laughed.

"Sheriff," said Walton, "they're in cahoots with each other and that ain't legal."

"Well," said one of bidders, "neither was that tea party they threw in Boston some years ago, but somehow they got by."

"Hap," said the high bidder for the land, "you'd best get off my property before I ask the sheriff to run you off."

Again the men laughed, one of them pleading with the new owner, "Don't run me off, Dave. I have the best of intentions."

Walton gritted his teeth and stormed off.

That didn't stop the comments. "You used to be one of us before you went to work for the bank."

CHARLESTON'S HOUSE OF STUART

* * *

"Does Mama know Christian and I are in town?"

Rachel lay on the bed in the guest bedroom at Hartleigh's house, and since houses built before the Civil War had few closets, dressers and armoires dominated the walls. The upside was that bedrooms were generally ballroom size. At the end of the four-poster bed sat a cedar chest, and on it, Rachel's luggage.

Alexander, a Negro servant, his son Benjamin, and Luke and Christian had hauled the luggage upstairs, placing the Jenny Lind in the only open spot against the wall. Then Benjamin had taken off to notify her parents that Rachel had arrived, while Luke stood on the porch and chafed in a new suit purchased during a layover in Memphis.

From the porch Luke could see the Ashley River, and off to the east, ships entering and leaving Charleston Harbor. Luke had never seen the ocean before, but he had seen Lake Michigan when his family had once traveled to Milwaukee. The Atlantic Ocean went on and on, much like Lake Michigan.

A slender young girl stepped through the front doors: curly auburn hair, green eyes, and brown skin, but fashionably dressed as a flapper with the cloche hat, the Mary Janes, and a pair of tan gloves. All the fashionably dressed women Luke had seen at the train station had milk-white skin, but this girl was different, and her tanned skin intrigued him.

She stood, hands together, holding a sweater. "I'm Tessa Stuart and you're Luke, Christian's brother."

"Yes . . . yes."

She handed him the sweater and turned her back

to him. "Could you please?"

"Er . . . yes." He noticed her figure as he fitted the sweater on her shoulders. This Stuart girl was positively cute.

"Thank you."

Tessa stepped to the edge of the porch and looked up and down the street. Cars had parked on both sides of South Battery; taxis came and went, discharging and picking up passengers.

"Oh, where has that Benjamin gotten off to?"

"The Negro boy?"

"Yes."

"Mrs. Stuart sent him to fetch Rachel's mom."

Tessa's shoulders slumped. "Then I guess I'll have to wait."

"Wait for what?"

"I need an escort to the visitation."

This confused Luke. If one of his sisters wished to go somewhere, she would simply get to stepping. But Charleston appeared to have a lot more rules than Dairyland.

Tessa's face brightened. "You have on your mourning clothes—could you escort me?"

"Where?"

"To my grandfather's."

"How far is it?"

"Next door."

"Next . . . door?" Luke looked to the wrought-iron fence between the two houses.

"You wouldn't be gone long. But if it's too much to ask . . ."

"No, no," said Luke. "I can. I will."

"Then you can come back and escort your brother to the visitation."

"Escort my brother? My brother needs no escort."

"Oh, goody." Tessa took his arm and they went down the steps. "Because I have some people I want you to meet."

Hartleigh had wanted to remind Benjamin not to forget to check the Stuart visitation for Rachel's parents, but that very subject had ignited an argument so heated that Hartleigh had stopped before completing the stairs. She watched as Christian and Rachel argued all the way into the guest room. Hartleigh surmised that they had spent too much time on the sleeper and had probably reined in their emotions in the presence of Luke. Only when Christian came out of the guest room did Hartleigh finally finish the stairs to the second floor landing.

"Your brother is on the porch."

Christian shook his head as he passed by. "That wife of mine can be the biggest chowderhead."

"Don't worry. I'll take care of her."

At the bottom of the stairs, Christian looked up at her. "Thank you, Hartleigh. You're still the nicest of the lot."

Sitting on the side of the four-poster bed, Rachel huffed and puffed. She was red-faced.

Hartleigh rushed over. "Rachel, are you all right?"

"Honestly, sometimes that man makes me so angry."

"Rachel, please. You must calm down. I've sent for your mother."

At the mention of her mother, Rachel closed her eyes and began to take long, slow breaths. Her grandmother always said a person couldn't remain hot under the collar while taking long, slow breaths.

"Rachel?"

She opened her eyes and held up a hand. "I'm fine, fine."

"Then lie down."

Rachel did as requested, but with some assistance from Hartleigh.

"Katie flew in this afternoon with one of her boys. Cousin Jimmy brought the other two down on the train." Hartleigh almost mentioned the visitation but caught herself.

There came a knock at the door.

"Come in," said Rachel, struggling to breathe.

Katie stuck her head inside. "Good to have you back in Carolina. The boys will be going with us, so get some rest."

"Thank you."

"See you in the morning."

The door closed.

"Thank you," said Rachel, "for all you've done."

"Think nothing of it." Hartleigh took a seat on the edge of the bed.

"I was sorry to hear about Sue Ellen's baby."

"Well, we still have a problem there."

Rachel's eyebrows rose. "Up to her old tricks, is she?"

"I don't think she wanted a family as much as you and I."

"Has James spoken to her?"

"Constantly."

"And she's not listening."

"Well, she is a Stuart."

"Do tell," said Rachel with a laugh. "Have you whipped your Stuart into shape?"

"You know, things change when you marry into the Stuart family."

"I know, I know. Franklin could never shine around James. Now look at him. Still single and number three on my list."

"After . . . ?"

"Daddy and Mama. Who are my candidates for Franklin?"

"Nell Ingram comes to mind."

"The one with the meddlesome parents?"

Deftly, Hartleigh changed the subject. "Charleston's not changed while you've been gone. The party's still going, but we now have soup lines."

"Lines formed by those who believed in an eternal boom. They should've put something away for a rainy day."

"Rachel, people are going hungry."

"Then they can return to the farm." Rachel held up her cracked and reddened hands. "I did."

Hartleigh tried to take her hands, but Rachel pulled them away.

"James says too many people have moved to the cities for this to be a quick recovery. He's afraid we're in for a long, hard slog, especially if Europe collapses."

"What does Europe have to do with us?"

"American banks have a lot of money invested there." Hartleigh had been cradling her tummy when she started. "Oh!"

"Kick?" asked Rachel, grinning.

"James says it's a boy for sure."

Rachel rubbed her tummy. "At least I've got two chances at getting it right. Belles do run to twins."

SIX

James Stuart was an eleventh generation Charlestonian and a direct descendant of the original James Stuart from Scotland. Contrary to what people believed, the mother of the original James Stuart did not have strong ties to the Scottish Highlands. As a young woman, she'd been kidnapped from her Protestant family while farming in one of the valleys, and when her Highlander "husband" fell in battle, a battle in which the Highlanders were bested by a regiment of battle-hardened redcoats, the surviving members of the clan returned to the Highlands to lick their wounds and divide up the women.

One of the women was Mary Stuart; her son was to be raised by his Catholic uncle. But after serving the men more whiskey than they could hold, and tolerating being slapped on the backside, being pinched and fondled, Mary packed a bag, gathered her son, and fled the Highlands.

Mary, however, did not return to central Scotland but disappeared into the bustling city of Glasgow. In Glasgow, Mary found work as a barmaid and occasional whore, and for this reason James grew up on the water instead of a farm soaking up much more education than one would normally expect.

The Scots were the most literate nation in Europe, and when the Acts of Union joined Scotland and England, access was granted to any Scot to go anywhere in the United Kingdom, including the American colonies—where James quickly learned that the second sons of Barbadian landowners controlled Charles Towne. James figured he had a better chance for success if he served on the Spanish Main under Captain Hornigold and alongside Edward Teach, otherwise know as Blackbeard.

When the king offered a pardon, James returned to Charles Towne, sailing a ship given to him by Captain Hornigold. There, he married Nelie Belle, and the Belle family became entwined with the Stuarts at the very beginning of the city.

Jeb, Senior, was laid out in the reception room (first room on the right as you came through the front door), and a long line of Stuarts greeted everyone who came to pay their respects.

Sue Ellen planned to move back in, but James wasn't so sure. With their mother so distraught, who would keep an eye on his sister? Perhaps he should ask Aunt Jo to stay over for a few weeks.

No. That wouldn't be fair to the rest of the family. Aunt Jo could be difficult, to say the least, so James remained silent as a servant was dispatched to pack Sue Ellen's clothing and toiletries and bring them home.

After the visitation, the Stuart men planned to meet in the study while Aunt Jo would supervise the help in clearing plates, cups, and uneaten food from the parlor, dining room, and reception area. Sue Ellen and Tessa would take Eileen Stuart upstairs and prepare her for bed.

When he had come through the line, Christian explained that he, Rachel, and his youngest brother had been on a train for the last thirty hours, and while Rachel did not appear to be suffering anything more than exhaustion, he was taking no chances.

Before he could move on, James took Christian's arm. "Don't leave. I want to speak with you."

"No, Christian," corrected Hartleigh from a chair in the reception line, "check on Rachel's condition, then, if Doctor Rose agrees, you can return to the party."

Christian glanced at James but nodded to Hartleigh.

"And don't forget to take a piece of cake." Hartleigh pointed to the dining room. "Devil's food is one of Rachel's favorites."

To the women who followed Christian through the line, Hartleigh asked, "Could I speak with you about the soup kitchen?" And since all the women lived south of Broad, they readily agreed to speak with her before leaving the visitation.

In the dining room, Georgiana spied Christian and moved to intercept him before her son-in-law reached the buffet.

Taking his arm, she asked, "Where's Rachel?"

"Oh, Mrs. Belle, good to see you again."

"Yes, yes, very nice to see you, too, but where's my daughter?"

"Doctor Rose is with her, but she'll be fine."

"Eight months pregnant and you allowed her to travel?"

"Actually, thirty hours ago we were in Wisconsin. There are nonstop trains between—"

"I don't care about timetables. I care about my daughter's health. Now, if you'll excuse me I must go to her."

Christian glanced at the food brought in by the neighbors: cold rice salad with English peas, ham-asparagus rolls, boiled shrimp on a bed of ice, baked ham, shrimp creole, and piles of biscuits. For sweets you could choose from benne wafers, charlotte russe, apple-pecan torte, ambrosia in a crystal bowl, or devil's food cake. Also on the table was one of Christian's favorites: she-crab soup. If there was one thing you could say about Charlestonians, they sure knew how to eat.

"I was returning to the house, Mrs. Belle. May I accompany you?"

"I'll just get my wrap."

Seeing how easily Tessa was helping Luke mix with the young people of Charleston, Christian went to the table and wrapped a slice of devil's food cake in his handkerchief. On the way to and from the table, several people, mostly tight, encouraged Christian to "have a little drinkie" from their flask. After all, Aunt Jo was in town.

His mother-in-law returned from the study with her fox fur coat and allowed Christian to put the garment over her shoulders. Christian only wore a business suit. There would have to be snow on the ground before any Wisconsinite would seriously consider wearing a topcoat.

Dr. Rose had finished his examination. Rose said Rachel would be up and around in a few days, but he wanted her to remain in bed for the next seventy-two hours. He'd return to check on her tomorrow, and he did not want to find her out of bed.

Once Dr. Rose and Christian left, a servant and Georgiana helped Rachel out of her clothing and into a nightgown. After a trip to the bathroom, Rachel was tucked under the covers and the servant dismissed. Then Rachel took a tiny bit of laudanum and downed it with a glass of water.

She made a face. "Well, that makes it official."

"The water tastes different in Wisconsin, my dear?" asked Georgiana.

Rachel placed the glass on the nightstand next to the slice of devil's food cake. "Christian calls Charleston's water 'beach water.' "

Georgiana took a seat on the side of the bed and gripped one of her daughter's hands. "You really thought you would attend the visitation tonight?"

"Mama, the moment I returned to Charleston I began to accumulate social obligations. Actually, I probably accumulated obligations while I was still up north."

"Your obligation is to your unborn children, not Charleston."

Rachel wasn't so sure.

Her mother was examining the red, rough hand with the broken nails and lack of polish. Strange, thought Georgiana. Rachel's generation made a fetish of painting their nails—psychiatrists attacked it as a form of self-mutilation, but Georgiana's generation viewed nail polish as another attack on Charleston society, as fewer and fewer young women wore gloves.

"My Lord, what has happened to your hands?" Georgiana reached across to pull her daughter's other hand from under the covers.

Rachel pulled the first hand away and slipped it under the covers. "On a farm everyone pitches in."

"Did Doctor Rose see your hands?"

"Of course, Mama." Rachel inclined her head toward a glass jar of lotion on the nightstand. "I'm to keep my hands out of water and apply that lotion three times a day."

"Well, it appears your hands didn't break out while up north."

"When working on a farm there's no time for a nervous condition."

"Your husband allowed you to travel?"

"It was a spur of the moment thing," said Rachel, remembering her embarrassing fall in the Andersens' kitchen. She colored slightly.

"I would think so." Georgiana scanned the room. "Do you have everything you need?"

"I'm fine, Mama. I just wanted to be with you when the babies arrive."

Georgiana smiled and brushed back an unruly strand of hair that had fallen across her daughter's brow. "I'll be here, my dear, even if I too must move in with the Stuarts."

"Well, let's hope it doesn't come to that."

There was a knock at the door and Hartleigh came in with a bowl of soup, a spoon, and a napkin. "I just returned from the visitation and wanted to bring this up before Rachel went to sleep. Everyone sends their best and can't wait to see you."

Georgiana fitted the napkin around her stepdaughter's neck. "Rachel's in no condition to receive guests."

Hartleigh gave the bowl to Georgiana. "Well, Mrs. Belle, I'll let you determine that, but give us tomorrow and let's see how it goes."

"Thank you," said Rachel, smiling up at Hartleigh.

Georgiana began to spoon feed the soup to her stepdaughter.

"Chicken noodle," said Hartleigh.

"Delicious," commented Rachel. "Thank you."

"She's taken some laudanum," said Georgiana between spoonfuls.

"Probably the best thing for her." Hartleigh leaned over and kissed Rachel on the forehead. "So glad to have you back in Charleston." She gestured at the cord dangling from the ceiling. "Just ring if you need anything. Molly said she would remain downstairs until midnight." She pointed at the nightstand. "And use the hand bell if you need me."

At the door, she faced them again. "Cousin Katie is across the hall with Jimmy and their boys, though I believe the boys will sleep downstairs with Luke."

"Rachel," suggested her mother, "you may wish to have your husband sleep down there too. You'll be much more comfortable."

Rachel shook her head. "Christian's the only reason I survived Wisconsin. Every night he held me until I fell asleep."

"Very well, my dear. It was just a suggestion."

"Good night, Rachel," said Hartleigh from the bedroom door. She clasped her hands over her abdomen, then grinned. "I'm giddy over the fact that we shall soon fill up this house with babies."

* * *

Eugene Roddey was sitting on the back porch of his clapboard house and polishing off his last bottle of whiskey when his cousin pulled into the yard, killed the pickup's engine, got out, and ambled over.

The cousin scanned the porch. Nothing but dead soldiers, but all lined up in an orderly fashion. "Any more in the house?"

Roddey shook his head. "Warehouse closed today. Started early."

A woman's voice came through the screened door. "Started after breakfast. Actually, he drank his breakfast."

Roddey raised his glass. "The king is dead! Long live the king!"

"Shame on you. Mister Stuart was always good to you."

"Shut up, woman!"

After they finished squawking, the cousin asked, "You still got the key to the warehouse?"

"Yeah," said Roddey, shakily getting to his feet.

From inside the house, the woman said, "If you're smart, you'll take along a thermos of hot coffee and try to sober him up."

SEVEN

In the study, Alexander mixed drinks and used tongs to retrieve ice cubes from a silver bucket while Lewis Belle, attorney for the Stuart family, wondered what James had in mind for the three men sitting in the rear of the room: Christian Andersen, the Yankee who had married Rachel Belle; Prescott Mitchell, the engineer who went everywhere in a wheelchair; and Luke Andersen, Christian's younger brother.

Lewis had noticed the strong interest taken in Tessa Stuart on the part of Luke Andersen. Lewis's youngest daughter had been here earlier, but curiously, though his daughter was a true beauty, she had not been able to pry Luke away from Tessa.

His wife counseled Lewis to let it be. "It's their turn to manipulate lovers, fall in love, or have catfights," she'd said.

Lewis Belle, a stout man with pale skin, blue eyes, and raven hair, was Rachel and Franklin Belle's uncle.

Tessa was the only daughter of Jeb, Junior, and a mother who had died of polio; her maternal grandparents had succumbed to the Spanish flu. As a consequence, the girl had nowhere to live. She could not go to sea with her father, and since her deceased grandfather had been a wife beater, that made the Stuart home off-limits. For this reason, Tessa had been raised at Ashley Hall, thereby getting a fine education, but still it wasn't home. Now, with the death of her grandfather, there was hope that Tessa could move in with her grandmother, thus regaining some normalcy in her life.

Christian had returned from escorting Georgiana to James's house. To Christian's way of thinking, there was something odd about that relationship. Why hadn't he and his wife gone to Rachel's to stay? Could it be that Rachel's father was still upset over his daughter marrying a Yankee? Mr. Belle certainly had avoided him during the visitation.

Christian and Luke were introduced to several people in the study by Tessa, and Christian became reacquainted with the crippled Prescott Mitchell. Christian had no idea what this meeting was about or why he and Luke had been included. He accepted both a scotch and a warm welcome from Alexander while Luke and Tessa were given lemonades. The two young people sat next to each other in folding chairs in the rear of the study, with Tessa carrying the burden of the conversation.

Last into the room was Aunt Jo, a member of the Woman's Christian Temperance Union, a champion of women's suffrage, and a born-again Christian. Jo had been a victim of one of the last arranged marriages in Charleston. She had married into the

Strom family of Edgefield County, and accompanying her today to her brother's funeral was the recently appointed superintendent of education for Edgefield County, Strom Thurmond.

While Jo organized and supervised the visitation and funeral, young Strom worked the room and later those at the funeral. When Jo appeared in her brother's study, the men hid their drinks, snubbed out their cigarettes, and Alexander stepped in front of the small bar.

Clearing her throat to make sure she had everyone's attention, Jo said, "This is a historic opportunity for this family. The death of my brother means the good Lord has other plans for this family and is telling us not to continue down this path of wickedness."

No one spoke. No one said a word. It was best to let Aunt Jo get off her chest whatever was on her mind.

After looking each man in the eye, she continued. "I can't say that I, alone, can end this wickedness, but I have done my part." She held up some keys and jangled them. "I changed the locks on the warehouse doors."

This set off howls of protests from the men, but before anyone could stop her, Jo was out of the study, shutting the door behind her.

Jeb, Junior, went after her, but Lewis called him back by jangling his own pair of keys. "This is our set."

The room broke into laughter, drinks were brought out, cigars and cigarettes relit, and the keys to the warehouse tossed to Jeb, who tossed them to Cousin Jimmy, who tossed the keys to James, who sat behind his father's desk. James dropped the keys onto the desk and returned to smoking a cheroot and staring at the half-empty glass of bourbon in front of him.

Jeb, Junior, handed his glass to Alexander for a refill. Before the Volstead Act, Junior had been a charter boat captain, but with the advent of Prohibition, he began to make more profitable runs to the Bahamas and Cuba. When the Coast Guard started seizing boats, his father had a two-mast ship built to haul contraband liquor to a point just outside the twelve-mile limit. From there a fleet of mahogany runabouts ran the last twelve miles, leaving the Coast Guard's cutters in their wake.

"It's all I can do to handle the transportation end of this operation." Jeb was ten years older than James and barely knew his younger brother or sister. He had spent his life at sea, and long before the enactment of the Volstead Act that had created Prohibition. "I vote for James."

Jeb was as dark as any Negro, had a grizzled face, and hair pulled back into a ponytail. With a scar running up one cheek, a souvenir from a life along the waterfront, Junior looked like a hobo stuffed into a business suit for the night. He had loosened his tie and now downed much of his drink in one swallow. Jeb's reputation as a drinker was equal to his late father's.

"I second the motion," said Cousin Jimmy from Greenville. Cousin Jimmy had begun the upstate end of the business by selling guns to the Scots-Irish, and later he sold liquor to just about anyone in the overwhelmingly dry counties of the upstate.

"Lewis, what do you say? You have a vote in this."

Anyone who contributed to the well-being of the House of Stuart always had a vote, though Lewis Belle rarely spoke unless asked a question.

James looked at Alexander. The Negro nodded and no one contradicted the fact that Alexander also had a vote. Outside, children ran up and down the hall, shrieking, shoes clicking on hardwood floors.

James straightened up in his father's chair. "I became a civil engineer to avoid working in the family business."

"Yeah," said Jeb, "you complicated your life and now you're paying for it."

James's eyes flickered at his older brother.

"I didn't go to any fancy school or aspire to live in a big house. I kept my dreams simple: me on a boat. Didn't want anything more, wasn't going to accept anything less."

James glanced at his niece. Tessa had lost her usual poker face and sobbed quietly into a handkerchief. Cousin Jimmy crossed the room and held Tessa's shoulder as she leaned into his hip and sobbed.

"That's what's wrong with you people," said Jeb, "you want the folks of Charleston to think well of you, but we'll always be bootleggers and our children and grandchildren will always be the descendants of bootleggers. Daddy kept his job at the bank so people would think better of him, but even that didn't work. Daddy was like every Stuart—a pirate at heart."

"Why the speech?" asked Cousin Jimmy from where he stood with his hand on Tessa's shoulder.

"Because you're a natural born salesman, Jimmy, and I'm a sailor. James has reconciled himself to the fact that he's a first-class planner."

One by one, family members and guests turned to the man sitting behind the desk.

But Jeb wasn't through. "For the last two years I've watched that bridge grow until it spanned the Cooper, and along the way I learned that my little brother was the site engineer. Makes a man proud to know his brother had a hand in building that bridge, ugly as it is. But most importantly, the bridge came in under budget."

Jeb toasted his brother. "To you, James. You can do this job. The family's depending on you." And he downed the remainder of his drink.

Everyone's attention again turned to James.

"Well?" asked Cousin Jimmy.

"I'm thinking about it. I'm thinking about it." But to James it felt as if his father were reaching out of his grave to direct his life once again.

"What's there to think about?" asked Jeb. "It's always been a three-man operation. I'm the importer, Cousin Jimmy distributes, and you run the warehouse."

"And you are way behind at the warehouse," commented Jimmy. "Some of my customers are getting restless."

James snubbed out the cheroot. "Okay, I'll do it, but I make all the decisions because I'll know all aspects of the business."

Cousin Jimmy considered this. Lewis Belle and Alexander were already nodding, so Jimmy voted for his cousin, too.

"Good," said Jeb, heading for the door. "I have a hot dame and a cold beer waiting and both are changing temperature."

The men in the library laughed.

"Aren't you forgetting something?" asked Cousin

Jimmy. He stood aside so Jeb could see his daughter.

"Oh, yeah." Jeb motioned to the girl. "Come on, kid."

Tessa sprang to her feet and raced after him, tears gone, face filled with anticipation.

Luke watched her go. For some reason, Tessa's leaving produced a sense of loss in Luke he did not fully understand.

Lewis gestured at those sitting in the rear of the room. "I assume you have a position in mind for these young gentlemen?"

Everyone looked to the blond man and his brother and the one in the wheelchair.

"Prescott and Christian helped build the bridge across the Cooper. I thought I might throw some work their way."

"Fine with me," said Lewis. James Stuart was the best judge of talent he had ever known, though he had misgivings about the man in the wheelchair.

"The problem is: I still want to know who killed my father."

The room went silent.

"James," said Lewis, "your father hit his head, fell off the pier, and drowned."

"There could be more to it than that."

"When you can prove an alternate theory, call the police."

James set his jaw. "I will."

Lewis stepped to the bar and put down his glass. He faced James as Alexander rebuilt his drink. "You have the chief of police in your pocket right now, but the moment you ask the chief to do his job, you'll appear at the top of any list of suspects. You and your father had some terrible public rows. Do you really have time for that now?"

For a long moment, James said nothing, then, "All right, I'll consider it later."

"Good," said Cousin Jimmy, snatching the keys off his uncle's desk. "Lewis, besides you and Aunt Jo, who else has these keys?"

"Roddey, the warehouse manager."

"Then I suggest a trip to the warehouse so we can learn how blind our loyal employees are robbing us."

EIGHT

At the warehouse along the Cooper, Alexander pulled back one of the heavy wooden doors, turned on the lights, and the Stuart party entered a brick building filled with a fleet of trucks and stacks of paper-wrapped furniture. Beyond the trucks and furniture were cartons of liquor as far as the eye could see. But you couldn't see the hooch unless you passed through the row of trucks and the stacks of furniture covered in dust.

As they headed for the office, Lewis Belle tapped a stack of cartons beside a truck. "Jeb's last haul."

"I'm surprised anything's still here," said Cousin Jimmy, "since they all know Uncle Jeb passed."

James looked around. "Anyone working today?"

"Probably closed out of respect for your father," said Lewis.

"There's a light on at the far end of the warehouse that I didn't turn on," said Alexander. The Negro headed in that direction.

James turned to Lewis, "Would you accompany Alexander?"

"Very well."

"Luke and I will tag along, too," said Christian, "if that's all right with you, Mister Belle."

"Certainly, but call me 'Lewis.' You married my niece and you're family now." He looked at Luke. "That rule doesn't apply to you, son, until you reach your majority."

Luke rolled his eyes. Southerners had so many rules.

In the office, which was glassed from halfway up, James flicked on a light. The room was bisected by a low railing, behind which sat a mahogany desk with a telephone. Behind the desk was a matching mahogany credenza. Off to the right was a bunk bed, to the left a table with another phone. To reach the far desk, you pushed your way through a low wooden gate. Chairs sat in front of the desk and a dusty Chubb safe stood in one corner.

Prescott stopped his wheelchair beside the bed with another bed stacked on top of it. "What the devil's this?"

"A bunk bed," said Cousin Jimmy, pushing his way through the low gate and into the rear section of the office. "I purchased one for the two younger boys. Katie doesn't much care for it. She says it gives them more room to roughhouse."

"Hmm," said Prescott, running his hand up and down a bedpost.

James was shuffling through paperwork when Alexander, Lewis, Christian, and Luke returned. As usual, Luke was bug-eyed at his surroundings and found the bunk bed especially fascinating. Through the half-glass walls, they saw the foreman, Roddey, trailing behind the others, clipboard in his hand.

"Who?" asked James of Lewis Belle.

"Roddey. He's here with two of his brothers, or cousins. It really doesn't matter. I asked him to wait outside."

Those in the office stared through the half-glass wall. Roddey saw this and slowed to a stop.

"Do the brothers or cousins work here?" asked James.

Lewis shook his head.

"And neither does the foreman any longer," said Jimmy, getting to his feet from where he'd been trying to open the safe.

Lewis looked to James for confirmation.

"Perhaps we should keep him on the payroll until I've learned the business," suggested James.

"It'd seem that the smarter play would be . . ." Jimmy's voice trailed off as he remembered his cousin's condition for joining Stuart and Company.

James smiled. "In for a penny, in for a pound."

"Okay, you're the boss. What do you want me to do?"

"I want you to load two of the most dependable trucks with whatever stock you need. Everyone will pitch in. While you're doing this, Alexander will fetch your luggage and the two younger boys from the house. You can leave tonight."

"I'll miss the funeral. Katie will raise hell."

James shrugged.

"Okay. You're the boss."

"Take Luke with you. The trucks have a bed behind the seats and your boys can sleep there. Luke, can you drive a truck?"

"Sure," said the boy sitting up on the bunk bed.

"Good. Alexander's wife will put together some food. Just tell her what you need."

"I'll need some guns. I didn't bring any."

"Alexander," said James, "do you know where the key to the gun cabinet is at the house?"

The black man nodded.

"And please don't forget the ammo," added Cousin Jimmy.

"I'm not comfortable with Luke doing something where he needs a weapon," said Christian. "I'll go instead."

James shook his head. "I want you to learn the warehouse routine. You did excellent work on the east side of the bridge. Every nut and bolt was accounted for and reached its proper destination."

"Christian," Jimmy assured him, "my boys will be on those trucks, too. You have nothing to worry about."

"I worry about what my mother will think if any harm comes to Luke."

His brother put in his two cents. "I can drive a truck. I've been doing it for years."

"Luke, that's not all they're asking you to do."

Alexander said, "I'll go."

But Jimmy was still pitching Luke. "We have our own gas pump in the courtyard, and we send out dummy trucks with any convoy. Nobody knows when we leave unless they're standing across the street, and that building belongs to us, too. Once they reach Goose Creek, the empty trucks return to the warehouse."

James gestured at the phone. "Call the highway patrol and get an escort. That should make Christian feel better."

It didn't.

Lewis placed a call to his contact inside the highway patrol substation. After that, Jimmy called Alexander's wife and ordered a picnic basket. He also told her to have Molly pack the younger boys' suitcases.

"And throw my suitcase into the truck along with any luggage of Luke Andersen."

"Do you have any idea when my husband will be home tonight?" asked Pearl.

"No idea at all," said Jimmy. "The warehouse is a mess, and Alexander's the only Negro in a sizable party of white men."

Pearl grunted and hung up.

Christian huddled with his brother in a corner. "You don't have to do this, Luke. You can still go home."

But Luke wanted to remain in Charleston. He wanted to know why Tessa Stuart had been crying during the family meeting and if there was anything he could do about it.

"I'll be fine. I just want to know how well Captain Stuart pays."

"He'll take care of you. He did that for me when I worked on the bridge, but you'll have to bust your butt."

"I'm not afraid of hard work."

"Ma will kill me if anything happens to you."

"It can't be any more dangerous than what's happening back home between the milk farmers and the cheeseheads."

Christian shrugged, then nodded his okay to James when the brothers faced him again.

To Prescott, James said, "I need someone to run this office."

"I studied engineering at Georgia Tech, not office management." Prescott gestured at his useless legs. "You're taking advantage of me because I'm a cripple."

"Not at all. Turner Logan's found an opening. It's a draftsman's position. You can rebuild your career from there."

"I was a draftsman the whole time I worked on the Cooper River Bridge. I think I'll pass."

"Suit yourself, but Stuart and Company is vulnerable to a raid by revenuers or an attack by the competition. If we get through the night, I want everything out of here in the next two days."

"That's a lot of rolling around."

"That's Christian's job. He runs the warehouse. You run the office. Just tell him what you need, or what a customer needs, and he'll be responsible for moving it out the rear door."

"That's worse than a draftsman, being stuck in this office all day."

"And nights. Bootleggers operate in the dark."

"No," said Prescott, shaking his head, "I don't think so."

"Then don't miss the truck picking up Jimmy's kids and their luggage. Alexander will drop you off at your and Polly's apartment."

Prescott extended his hand over the railing. "So you're not sore?"

James stepped around the large desk and shook hands. "Of course not." He knew Polly's father sent money each month and Prescott didn't have to work for a living.

Prescott wheeled around and headed for the door. Lewis opened his mouth to object, but James shook his head.

At the door, Prescott faced them again. "By the way, what were you paying?"

"Fifty a week against a percentage of the take."

"I don't understand—"

"The Stuarts started out as pirates," explained Lewis.

"Privateers," corrected James.

"Privateers then. The ship received a share like all the men."

"What percentage?"

"Depends on the number of hands, but in this case probably a little less than ten percent."

"That includes both Alexander and Luke," added James.

"Ten percent of the take? How much will that be?"

Lewis laughed. "A lot."

Cousin Jimmy hung up the phone, shook hands all around, and then gave James a farewell hug. "Sorry about your daddy. Good luck."

James nodded.

Prescott had returned to the low gate. A sizable pile of money wouldn't get him a new pair of legs, but it did mean a lot less annoyance for the rest of his life. Maybe he'd even get a ramp or an elevator to allow him to come and go as he pleased.

"The first job is to get this safe opened," said James.

"Do you have the combination?"

"Ask Roddey."

Prescott rolled to the door, opened it, and called to Roddey.

Lewis lowered his voice to ask, "A cripple can work in a warehouse?"

James shrugged. "Give you someone to look down on instead of the Negroes."

"Aw, come on, James."

"We're just lucky a Belle will condescend to work with us pirates."

"Privateers," corrected Lewis. "I still have my standards."

Everyone laughed, which put off the foreman as he entered the office.

"It wasn't what it looked like, Captain Stuart. We had a delivery to make, and nobody came in today, you know, on account of your daddy, God rest his soul." The foreman was a short, stocky man. His sleeves were rolled up revealing tattoos and muscles. He wore workman's clothing and boots. "Sorry for your loss." The foreman looked around, finally fixing on the man in the wheelchair.

"Thanks for your concern," said James. "I need two of the most dependable trucks loaded tonight. Can you and your cousins help us do that?"

"Of course."

"Your relatives aren't employed here," said Lewis.

"I was going to give them a few bucks."

James pulled out his wallet and counted out ten dollars in singles. "You must pay the men fairly or they'll steal from you."

The other men looked at each other. This was how you treated an obvious thief? And would any of that money actually get to Roddey's cousins?

"I'll remember that." He stuffed the money in his pocket.

"Give everyone tomorrow off, but tell them to report here after dark."

"Yes, sir."

"Invite them to the funeral, even if you have to go door to door with your cousins. At a time like this we need to know who our friends are."

"I'm sure everyone will be there."

"That sounded like a guarantee." James gestured at the safe. "Now, before you go, can you open the safe?"

Roddey came through the gate, knelt in front of the safe, and started to dial the combination, then stopped.

He stood up. "I'm sorry, Captain Stuart. I don't know the combination." He gestured at the attorney. "Perhaps Mister Belle."

Lewis rolled off the wall, walked over to the safe, knelt, and spun the dial.

"That load you were taking out tonight with your brothers," asked James, "is it ready to go?"

"Cousins, sir. Er . . . almost."

"Well, hop to it! We've got a lot of work to do."

"Yes, sir." Roddey glanced at Prescott. "Captain Stuart, are you bringing in someone to work in the office."

"I am."

"But my mother usually—"

"It's not right to give a job to a woman with so many men out of work. What were you paying her?"

"Six dollars a week."

"Six dollars," muttered Lewis, swinging open the safe to reveal several journals. He thumbed through the journals and pulled out the most recent.

Again James took out the money clip and peeled off more bills. He handed them to Roddey. "Tell your mother she's retired, and if she needs references, she'll get them, but the work must go to the heads of households."

Roddey thanked James, left the office, and walked

the length of the warehouse. Before he opened the rear door to the courtyard, he was thumbing through a stack of manifests on a clipboard. He found his cousins smoking and lounging on the tailgate of a Chevy pickup.

"Well, are we caught?" asked one of the men. The courtyard was surrounded by a brick wall and had another set of large doors exiting onto the adjoining street. A gas pump stood in the middle of oil-soaked ground against the far wall.

Roddey handed a manifest to his cousins. "We are if this doesn't match with what's already in the truck."

The cousins looked at Roddey, then each other, and finally slid off the tailgate,

One of them snatched the manifest. "We'll make it right."

"You'd better. Stuart's already fired my mother."

The men looked at him from the rear of the truck. One asked, "Captain Stuart didn't gave your ma nothing?"

Roddey nodded. "Right, and she's still expected to be at the funeral tomorrow."

"Well, the devil with that."

"If you're not there, you don't have a job."

"Well, then," said the cousin, "Captain Hard-ass shouldn't walk down too many dark alleys or someone just might try to learn how tough he really is."

James called Christian into the office. Once the Yankee had closed the door, James tapped the ledger Lewis Belle had laid on the desk in front of him.

"This will be your bible regarding what liquor goes where." James gestured around the room. "If you've noticed, there are no file cabinets. Very little of this operation is written down. It's up to you and Prescott to pull everything together and empty the warehouse. Do you have any qualms about being a bootlegger?"

"Beggars can't be choosey."

"The Empire State Building is hiring. Sue Ellen's husband told me."

Christian shook his head. "My wife is a Charlestonian, born and bred."

Lewis laughed. "Another Yankee snared by a belle."

Christian smiled. "Can't argue with that."

"At any moment, you and I could be called away for the birth of our sons. We must get this operation up and running before someone sticks his nose into our business. I'll be at the funeral tomorrow. Everyone else works."

"Me?" asked Lewis Belle.

"You most of all."

"Yeah," said Prescott with a laugh. "I'd say in a couple of weeks you're going to hate this place as much as I will."

At the visitation, Aunt Jo had impressed on Hartleigh that she was doing the Lord's work by serving soup at the church twice a day. "Just remember that those lines are God's way of reminding America that this great country has strayed from the path of righteousness."

With that in mind, Hartleigh summoned Pearl and Molly to her bedroom. "I've been ordered to bed by Doctor Rose. I was allowed to attend the visitation but that ends it."

"You stay right there, Miss Hartleigh," said Pearl.

"We'll take care of everything."

"I'm still worried about the soup kitchen."

"Miss Hartleigh," said Molly, "you should've never gone there in the first place. A lady serving riffraff just ain't right."

"It was the Christian thing to do, and since James will be involved in the family business, I plan to exact a tribute. I've already informed him that he'll have to double my household expenses if he's going to be coming home late." Hartleigh was familiar with her husband's work habits. While he was building the bridge, she'd hardly seen him.

"What do you want us to do?" asked Pearl.

"Is there any way one of you could help at the soup kitchen?"

The two Negroes looked at each other.

"Well," said Pearl, "I guess one of us could fill in for you."

Hartleigh smiled. "Thank you. Whatever you can do."

"Miss Hartleigh," said Molly, "there are Negroes going without. Whole families."

"Don't we send the church a hundred dollars every month?"

Glancing at her sister, Molly said, "I thought we might buy the groceries and deliver them ourselves. No more cash."

Nodding her understanding, Hartleigh said, "Then next time you order have the grocery include an extra sack of potatoes, a good-sized roast, a can of coffee, tins of tea, salt, pepper, and sugar. You select the vegetables."

NINE

After leaving everyone to their tasks, James and Lewis called on their main competitor in his speakeasy on Market Street.

"Where's your wife tonight?" demanded Vincenzo Petrocelli when James and Lewis approached the table where Petrocelli, his wife, and a bodyguard sat.

"At home in bed, I hope. She's eight months pregnant." James glanced at the bodyguard, a man with a bald head and no neck. "But if that's an example of your intelligence gathering, you need to find someone else to fill the position."

The bodyguard tried to get to his feet, but Petrocelli grabbed his arm and pulled him back down. "Sit down, Bruno!"

Rita Petrocelli turned on her husband. "Mrs. Stuart's eight months pregnant. You couldn't get me out of the house then." She looked to James. "How's the baby?"

"Kicks like a boy."

The band broke into a snappy number, demanding those in the audience return to the dance floor.

"Mrs. Petrocelli, would you care to dance?" James put his derby on the table.

The woman glanced at her husband. "Love to, but—"

"I don't dance," said Petrocelli.

His wife shrugged.

"You want to dance," said her husband, "dance with the lawyer while we talk."

Instead, Lewis took a seat. "My friend is here only as a courtesy. I'm the brains of the outfit."

Bruno laughed, then realized he was the only one laughing.

"Mrs. Petrocelli," said James, extending a hand, "if you'll do me the honor."

"Is this some kind of a joke?" asked the bootlegger.

"No joke," said James. "You need to talk business so the rest of us need to give you some privacy. Mister Belle speaks for Stuart and Company."

"I don't talk to underlings."

"So," said James, withdrawing his hand, "I'm to sit here and embarrass myself about a business I know little about?"

"It's your family business."

"I'm a civil engineer, not a liquor distributor." Again, James extended a hand to the man's wife. "If you have no objections."

Rita took her husband's arm. "Now remember, you owe me."

Vince shot her a look. *"I owe you?"*

"You promised me a dance or two tonight."

"That's when I thought Mrs. Stuart would be here."

James continued to hold out his hand.

"You want me to throw them out, boss?" asked Bruno.

"If you don't want us to dance—" started James.

"Oh, hell," shouted Petrocelli, "go dance!"

"Oh, goody!" Rita Petrocelli shoved her chair back and practically leaped to her feet.

Couples watched Rita take to the dance floor with James Stuart. None of the patrons could remember the last time anyone had danced with Rita Petrocelli.

"No slow dancing!" shouted her husband from where he sat.

The couple paid him no mind. The music called for a foxtrot and soon they were quickly moving around the crowded dance floor. Smoke filled the air, as did laughs and shouts. The idea that Charleston would dry up during Prohibition seemed almost laughable.

"Boss, you want me—"

"Go to the bar!"

"What?"

"Go to the bar and have a beer."

"Well, if you're okay with that."

"You heard me! Go to the bar."

"Okay, boss, okay. I'll be right over there."

"Just go!"

Petrocelli returned his attention to Lewis Belle. "People told me you were a big kidder."

"Well, you only go through life once."

"Somebody might take offense and shorten that life."

"Then I would say those people should lighten up."

"You want something to drink?"

Lewis shook his head. He knew Petrocelli was a

teetotaler. Instead, he took out a pack of Camels and offered one to the bootlegger.

Petrocelli leaned over, took the cigarette and the light from Lewis's lighter. Petrocelli straightened up, drawing the smoke down deep into his lungs, then blowing it out through his nose. "Well, you called this meeting."

Lewis took a drag off his cigarette and put it in an ashtray. "Nothing changes but one thing, well, two. Captain Stuart will not deal in dope."

Petrocelli leaned back in his chair. "You people south of Broad always had a little too much starch in your collar. What's the other thing?"

"Stuart and Company will no longer operate brothels. We asked for this meeting to see how soon you could take them over. I believe there are three, and you know where they're located."

"So, no dope and no whores. What do you want in return?"

"What you must understand is that Captain Stuart just finished building the bridge across the Cooper. The death of his father doesn't give him a chance to catch his breath. He needs to spend time with his wife and new baby but still learn the ropes of the business. That's what we want for the brothels: time."

Vince glanced at the dance floor. His wife looked like she was enjoying herself. Maybe he *should* learn how to dance. Returning his attention to Belle, he said, "You're serious about Stuart not knowing the business?"

"As you probably know, Captain Stuart earned several medals in the Great War."

"And that's supposed to impress me?"

"No." Lewis jerked his thumb at Bruno watching from the bar. "You're supposed to remember that when your thick-necked friend wants to do something really stupid."

"Bruno served in the war, too."

"And he was dishonorably discharged for beating prisoners. And they weren't even Krauts. They were our own soldiers."

"Well," said Petrocelli with an evil grin, "Bruno did come highly recommended."

"You need to keep Bruno on a tight leash during this transition."

"Relax, Belle. I can control him. God, but you SOBs are stuck on yourself."

"My kind view it as simply maintaining the social order."

"More likely your kind keeping a boot on the neck of my kind."

"I'm not concerned about people's feelings, only their stupidity. You have Captain Stuart's word that we will make this transition work."

"So I'm supposed to warn Bruno to keep his distance? Bruno might take that as a challenge."

"Oh, do as you wish, but keep in mind that those medals won during the Great War aren't the only reason Bruno should keep his distance." He picked up his cigarette and took a drag off it. "Do you know Prescott Mitchell, the engineer in the wheelchair?"

"I've seen him around town."

"Prescott thought he would impress Captain Stuart's sister by taking her to the top of the new Cooper River Bridge to initiate her into the One Hundred and Fifty-foot Club."

Vince laughed. "Rita heard about that club. She

wanted to join. I thought it was stupid."

"But you did join?"

"Sure. I don't turn down girls, even my wife."

"Sue Ellen was able to successfully fight off Prescott's advances, but Captain Stuart saw the bruises."

"So he put Mitchell in a wheelchair?"

"No," said Lewis, after another drag off his cigarette, "that was the doctor's doing. Stuart's the one who threw Mitchell off the Cooper River Bridge."

"Well, finally, I'm impressed." He rested his own cigarette in the ashtray.

Lewis did the same, then reached inside his coat pocket. At the bar, Bruno reached inside his.

Taking out a sheet of paper, Lewis asked, "Would you care to examine our customer list so we don't get our wires crossed?"

"Yeah, yeah, but I'm more used to dealing with Stuart's father." Taking out his glasses, Petrocelli added, "He wasn't too good to shoot the breeze with me." He held out the glasses before putting them on. "I only use these for reading."

Lewis tapped his chest. "Me, too."

Petrocelli put on the glasses, took the list, and said: "Uh-huh, uh-huh, uh-huh." He looked up. "I might have a problem with two or three of these."

"We just gave you three cathouses and bowed out of the dope trade, and you have a problem with my list?"

Petrocelli put away his glasses. "Yeah. There's that."

Lewis picked up his cigarette and took another drag. "So we're all set?"

The bootlegger gestured at his wife and James on the dance floor. "So, what's his problem?"

"Whorehouses and dope."

"But he'll distribute liquor."

"Forbidding the consumption of alcohol or gambling in a seaport makes absolutely no sense to Captain Stuart. The state failed to eliminate moonshine, and the Yankee government thinks it can succeed where South Carolina couldn't? Besides, when Prohibition ends, he can return to being a civil engineer."

Petrocelli laughed. "For that you'd need an amendment. Nah, Prohibition will go on forever."

"Then make sure you pay your taxes."

"What?" Petrocelli took the cigarette from his mouth. "Why's that?"

"That's how the G-men are going after Capone—for income tax evasion."

"You serious?"

"Mister Petrocelli, I'm a hundred percent with you on the amendment. It'll never pass, so I make sure I pay my taxes."

The dance concluded, and James and Rita returned to the table, as did the bodyguard from the bar.

"It was my pleasure, Mrs. Petrocelli," said James, scooting her chair under the table. "You don't know what you're missing. Your wife is an excellent dancer."

"Vince, Captain Stuart gave me the name of a fellow who can teach you how to dance."

Petrocelli snorted.

James looked at Lewis, who had gotten to his feet when Rita returned to the table. James joined his friend on the other side of the table, standing.

"Are we ready to go?"

"Mister Petrocelli agreed with me on every point."

"Hey, now, I didn't say that."

"Oh, I assumed you wouldn't look a gift horse in the mouth." Lewis held out his card. "Call me if there's anything I can do for you."

Petrocelli took the card. "I'll let you know, Belle."

"If you care to know, Captain Stuart wanted to tell the chief of police that he was free to close down those three bordellos, but I convinced him to meet with you. Closing down bordellos makes great headlines, and you can't have too many friends in high places, but there's that special relationship between your outfit and the House of Stuart."

Petrocelli nodded. "Lot of truth to that."

James asked Lewis. "Did you ask about the soup kitchens?"

"James, that's none of our business. People out of work need to get a job."

"It's my money so don't tell me how to spend it."

Lewis shook his head. "Not in front of these people."

Petrocelli scooted back. "Which people?" He stood up.

Lewis rolled his eyes.

The bodyguard joined his boss on his feet. Rita Petrocelli clutched her purse and pushed back her chair. She looked from her husband to James Stuart and back again. Petrocelli had his hand under his coat, but his bodyguard had actually pulled his weapon.

The room went silent, including the band. Waiters coming from the kitchen were quickly shushed by those at the tables. Everyone stopped and stared at the guy with the pistol.

"You want to apologize for that crack?"

James said, and rather icily, "We're not apologizing for anything unless he puts away that gun."

"Put away the gun, Bruno."

"But, boss—"

"Put away the gun!"

Reluctantly, the bodyguard did.

James gestured at Lewis. "My friend is a clod, Mrs. Petrocelli."

"Now, see here, James—"

"I apologize for any insult, and I'm terribly sorry if his comments marred our lovely experience on the dance floor." He turned to the attorney. "Lewis, are you willing to offer an apology?"

Lewis looked at those facing him across the table. "I meant no disrespect."

"And?" asked James.

Lewis stared at the table. "I apologize."

"Apology accepted," said Rita Petrocelli. "And, Captain Stuart, once again, thanks for the dance."

"My pleasure." James looked at Petrocelli. "My wife would like to know if you would pony up a thousand dollars for the soup kitchens."

"And why would I do that?"

"So you won't be thought of as a clod—like my friend here."

"James," protested Lewis, "please . . ."

"Bruno, the bar."

"But, boss—"

"The bar. Now!"

The bodyguard stuffed his pistol into a shoulder holster and returned to the bar.

"The thousand is just a start," explained James. "In the future, you and I will have to provide food and clothing for a lot of people, so make sure your wallet tends to open wide when you see me coming. Some of the warehouses may have to be converted into hotels for displaced families."

"I busted my butt to separate myself from those other bums—"

James gestured around the smoke-filled room. "And you've done a great job."

Lewis snorted.

Petrocelli's eyes quickly iced over. "Belle, I should shoot you myself, but I'd never rid Charleston of all you SOBs."

"Please ignore him, Mister Petrocelli. There are people starving, and you and I are the only ones who can do anything about it."

Lewis looked at his feet and shook his head.

Petrocelli saw this. "You don't agree, Belle?"

"I do not," said Lewis, looking up. "This good will gesture by Captain Stuart will only draw more people to the dole. The Panic was just that. People temporarily lost their minds, but sooner or later they'll find jobs. The stock market is already recovering."

"Then how do you explain the soup lines?" asked James.

Lewis shrugged. "The poor will always be with us."

James smiled at Petrocelli. "I told you he was a clod."

"James, would you stop that?"

"You can put us down for two thousand," said Rita Petrocelli. "I'd offer more, but I'm going to need the rest for dancing lessons."

In the car, Lewis said, "I don't like being treated like the help, James."

"Father never took you to meet Petrocelli, did he?"

"No," said Lewis rather slowly.

"Probably so you could honestly say that you'd never met the man. Think of how important that might've been if you'd ever had to appear in court."

"I see," agreed Lewis, who found this much easier to swallow than being called a clod.

"Where to next, James?" asked Alexander.

"The gin mill." So named for all the liquor cut there.

Alexander turned the car inland.

"So Petrocelli agreed to our customer list?"

"Well, you did give him three bordellos."

"What reason did you give for my irrationality?"

"I told him your wife's a prude."

James smiled out the window. "And I wouldn't have her any other way."

Hartleigh was reading when someone tapped at her door. She laid *The Great Gatsby* open across her swollen belly.

"Come in."

It was Molly. She said, "I wanted you to know that Benjamin just got back. He said he didn't leave the porch until he heard Miss Tessa turn the lock in the door."

"Very well." Hartleigh scribbled a note on a pad lying beside her on the bed. Rarely did people lock their doors, but three women lived in the house next door, and they should be encouraged to lock up at night.

Before leaving the visitation, Hartleigh had detailed Benjamin to watch over Tessa. Her father would've thought nothing of sending the girl home in a taxi, or worse, having an ordinary seaman escort her home. Totally unsuitable for a young Charleston lady.

"Please ask Pearl to consider allowing Benjamin to sleep next door until we work out some other arrangement. I know they'll make sure Benjamin does his homework and walks his sister to school each day."

"I'll ask her." Molly remained at the door.

"Yes?"

"Miss Tessa wanted to know if Luke Andersen got in tonight and where he was staying."

"Well, he's certainly not staying next door."

Molly laughed. "Good night, Miss Hartleigh." And she left the room, closing the door behind her.

Hartleigh returned to her reading. No matter the hour, she planned to be awake when her husband came home. She had a point to make.

TEN

Alexander left Charleston and drove into the countryside. Soon there was only the darkness of the surrounding farmland as they crossed over an offshoot of the Cooper River and then followed a recently paved road into a heavily wooded area. They met no one approaching from the opposite direction. This was the entrance to the gin mill, and over a mile long. Another road took the trucks away from here.

"How were you able to convince Petrocelli to take me seriously? I have no experience in the liquor trade."

"I told him you won a bunch of medals during the Great War, and that you threw Prescott Mitchell off the bridge when he insulted your sister."

James grunted.

Alexander chuckled.

"Well, now," said Lewis, "you did point out that Petrocelli's intelligence-gathering leaves a lot to be desired."

Men brandishing shotguns, rifles, and flashlights stepped out of the darkness and waved the Buick to a stop. Beams shot through the car, checking the driver and his passengers. Lewis rolled down his window to be better seen. A man recognized him and told the others to let the car pass.

A short time later, Alexander pulled into a turnaround in front of a huge, open-air barn. They were followed by a truck that continued around to the rear of the barn and lined up behind several idling trucks. The roar of a Cummins Diesel generator came from a large shed set off in the tree line as the Charleston power grid did not yet reach all of Charleston County.

"I hate this place," said James, getting out of the car. "I even hated the idea when my father told me about it over ten years ago."

He and Lewis left Alexander smoking a cigarette beside the car and walked through the two huge front doors where the interior of the barn was lit up like daylight. Boxes of liquor were being lifted by diesel-powered forklifts into the rear of trucks passing through. Several men remembered James from working on the bridge, stopped what they were doing, and came over and offered their condolences.

Alongside the line of trucks passing through the barn, bottles of whiskey were emptied into vats and mixed with raw alcohol, a good deal of water, and caramel for color. A touch of creosote gave the watered-down liquor a smoky flavor. Counterfeit labels were pasted on before the bottles were re-boxed and loaded onto trucks for the trip inland.

Where Stuart and Company made their money was in shipping large quantities of watered-down hooch over a network of newly paved roads leading into the midlands, and beyond that, the dry counties of the upstate. For this reason, the company maintained two lawyers in Columbia lobbying the legislature for more paved roads to the most out-of-the-way corners of the state.

Samuel Chase, who had once run the family bakery on Market Street, walked over and stuck out a hand. "Thanks for coming by, James. I know this is a tough time for you."

The three of them stepped into a small office so that James could be properly briefed. Ten years ago, Samuel had approached James's father about the profits to be made by running a distillery catering to those who didn't know their whiskey. Jeb's attitude didn't change when Samuel purchased a carton of whiskey and returned the following day with four cases of the same product, or so it seemed.

Jeb took one swallow and spit it out. "My God, Samuel, that's terrible! Who'd drink such swill?"

"Anyone who can't afford the more expensive stuff, and believe me, there's going to be a dearth of premium liquor in this state the longer Prohibition goes on."

Jeb, Senior, shook his head. "I don't know . . ."

Samuel gestured at the four cartons created from one carton of premium whiskey. "Well, let me know. You can always reach me at the bakery."

Jeb was still shaking his head and trying to wash the foul taste out his mouth with a decent Scotch when Roddey, who had watched the demonstration, asked, "What do I do with this stuff, Mister Stuart?"

"Throw it out!"

"Er . . . would it be okay if I took it home with me?"

"You're going to drink this swill?"

"No, sir. I thought I might sell it. You know, make a little money on the side."

"Something wrong with what I'm paying you to run this warehouse, Roddey?"

"Oh, no, sir, but I do try to keep my options open."

Less than a month later, Jeb, Senior, purchased the acreage outside Charleston and sent in a crew to build the huge, open-air barn with gravel-road access to Highway 78 North. A year later, the roads leading into and out of the gin mill were paved by the state.

James peered out the window as they were waved through by more armed guards with flashlights. "I dislike selling inferior goods," said James. "The reputation of Stuart and Company was not built on poor quality."

"Be that as it may, that barn makes more money than any other aspect of the business."

Peering into the darkness, James mumbled, "I know . . . I know." And once again, he felt the hand of his dead father reaching out of the grave and influencing his life.

The last stop was a building across the street from the police station. In front of the station, newsboys hawked papers by shouting tomorrow's headline: Major Bootlegger Possibly Murdered!

James stared at the boys across the street.

Lewis took his arm and guided him toward the door. "People don't do a lot of standing around in front of this building."

A young strawberry blonde looked up from the confession magazine she was reading, smiled, and buzzed them into the lobby.

"How's the boy?" asked Lewis.

"Can't wait to attend the Citadel. I'm going to hold you to your promise, Mister Belle." She waved them onto an elevator to the top floor, the fourth floor.

Once the elevator doors closed behind them, James asked, "Susan's still working at this hour?"

"She has a small child and no husband."

Riding up in the elevator, Lewis clapped James on the back. "Don't worry. It's the safest building in the city. The police are right across the street."

When the elevator doors opened, they found a man waiting for them. He frisked them, and finding no weapons, gestured down the hallway to a white-painted glass door with Stuart and Company lettering. A sign at the bottom of the glass, about halfway down the door, read: Ring buzzer for access.

Lewis did and a bell rang inside the room, then the door clicked and James followed Lewis through. Behind a desk sat a heavyset man wearing a business suit. A half-smoked cigarette lay in an ashtray, and on the desk, an automatic pistol along with a copy of *Riders of the Purple Sage*. On a console radio Duke Ellington played—live from the Cotton Club. There were no chairs other than the one the male receptionist sat in, his hands resting on the desk. Looped around the man's left thumb was a wire connected to the trigger of a double-barreled shotgun.

"Weapons?" he asked.

Lewis answered in the negative.

"Hands behind your head."

Lewis and James complied.

Only then did the receptionist slip the wire from his thumb and stand up. While James was being patted down, he glanced at the spot below the lip of the receptionist's desk. Two square inches of the wood were slightly off-color and made of papier-mâché to give clear range for the shotgun hidden there.

Satisfied, the receptionist stood aside and gestured to the door behind his desk. Through this door, they entered a large, dark room where the windows had been painted over.

Lights hung from the ceiling and metal shades reflected light onto the desks below them. Smoke was everywhere. Everyone was either counting money or taking bets over the phone. Occasionally, one of the men, who all wore visors, bowties, and garters around their shirtsleeves, carried a shoebox over to a floor-to-ceiling cage in the rear where he shoved it through a wire hatch; then, after receiving a receipt, the man returned to his desk.

No one paid the least bit of attention as Lewis led James back to the cage. In that cage sat a very small man behind a very large desk. Lewis had to pound on the frame to get his attention. The man stopped writing in a ledger, looked up, and rose from his chair. He was at the most five feet tall, and, like the other men in the room, his complexion was pasty white and he wore a green visor.

"Ah, yes, Mister Belle."

Lewis introduced James, and James looked around for a way to reach the man.

"No way in, Captain Stuart," said the short man, rather sheepishly. He fingered a key attached to his belt. "I have the only key."

Off to one side, a dumbwaiter labored to the fourth floor level and came to a stop. A man in the larger room, and near the dumbwaiter, left his desk and raised a small door in the wall. Soon he was dumping bags and envelopes from the dumbwaiter onto a waiting cart. Once the dumbwaiter was empty, a button was pushed and the dumbwaiter began its return journey to a lower floor. The small door was slid shut, and the man with the cart went around the room distributing the packets.

The short man cleared his throat. "Captain Stuart, I'll need to see some identification."

He directed the request to James, but it was Lewis who drew a passport from his inside jacket pocket. Lewis thrust the passport through the same slot used by the shoeboxes.

The short man compared the photo to James.

"You have my passport?" asked James of Lewis.

"Picked it up from Hartleigh when I took hers to have her name changed. You never know when newlyweds will want to sail for Havana. It does have the most beautiful beach in the hemisphere."

The short man returned the passport. "My condolences. I'll be at the funeral tomorrow."

"Thank you."

"Standard operating procedure is one-third of the proceeds to be returned to your brother, Jeb, so he'll have operating capital, one-third is deposited in banks overseas, and a third goes into local banks."

"How much is in gold?" asked James.

Lewis cut in. "Your father and I discussed that many times, but he never made a decision. There was simply too much money coming in, and sooner or later all that cash loses its value."

"Not for me, it doesn't." To the short man, he said, "The one-third that goes overseas—turn it into gold."

The short man made a note.

Lewis asked, "Where do we store it?"

"Switzerland, and get on it fast. When England goes off the gold standard, there's going to be a run on gold."

"England's going off the gold standard?" asked the man on the other side of the wire. "I thought it already was."

"Don't you read the papers?" asked James.

"Yes, but there's nothing in the papers about England going off the gold standard."

"But plenty about European countries who can't pay their debts. England alone owes over eight million, and most of that to us. Going off the gold standard is a license to print money."

Behind them, the room had gone quiet. Phones rang but went unanswered.

James explained. "During the Civil War, the Yankee government issued new money: greenbacks, making the demand notes obsolete. Now, Washington's done it again by printing these new smaller bills. Who's to say that's not another ploy to drive all the money out from under our mattresses and back into the banks? Banks that could fail any day now."

James raised a finger. "On that thought, put a man, full time, researching the soundest banks in the country. As he finds them, shift the one-third local money into those banks."

The man in the cage made another note. As he did, he said, "I don't understand why the government is involved in the economy. It's not like it's any of their business."

"You think you've got problems now, just wait until that new tariff goes into effect. Imports will go in the toilet and unemployment through the roof.

Matter of fact, the market crash was caused by the new tariff."

"But, James," argued Lewis, "Smoot-Hawley hasn't been sent to the president. It's still in committee."

"You don't think businessmen didn't see this coming? If RCA was $549 per share last year, who do you think was selling?"

After a long pause where the only sound was the incessant ringing of the telephones, a voice behind him said, "RCA."

James turned on the man. "And now RCA's sitting on piles of cash. Or their banks are."

"Then why," asked the short man in the cage, "are they not lending? Before the crash my sister's family wanted to buy a house, but none of the banks would give them a loan."

"The banks believed your sister and her husband were going to use that loan to play the stock market."

"But that's not true!" objected the short man. "They just wanted to buy a house."

"Well, tell them to hold on to whatever cash they have. Sooner or later there won't be enough money to go round."

"What?" asked more than one man.

"The Fed hasn't printed enough money to keep up with the demand of the Roaring Twenties. You have an expanding economy, you must expand the money supply. The Fed didn't."

James wagged a finger at them. "Always keep some cash under the mattress. The day is coming when the economy will run out of cash, and then everything will grind to a halt."

* * *

Hartleigh woke up when James dropped a shoe.

"Sorry. I was trying to be quiet."

"What time is it?"

"After midnight."

"Darling, the funeral's tomorrow. Please get some sleep."

After her husband returned from the bathroom, Hartleigh, half asleep, asked, "What kept you?"

"Just business, dear, just everyday business."

ELEVEN

After a luncheon and the funeral, and several more hours of additional receiving at the Stuart home under the watchful eye of Aunt Jo, the girlfriends decamped for Hartleigh's parlor for a smoke and a glass of sherry. While they were joking about Jo, Rachel Andersen lumbered downstairs in her robe and shook a copy of *Vanity Fair* at her upstate relative.

"Katie," raged Rachel, "this article is the most vicious attack on the Belle family since Sherman's men threatened to burn down Cooper Hill."

The other three girls looked to Katie, then back to Rachel. All were titillated as any Charlestonian would be at any family airing their dirty laundry in public.

The blonde on the loveseat took the cigarette from her mouth. "The article was heavily fact-checked," said Katie. "It is, after all, *Vanity Fair*."

Rachel threw the magazine at the loveseat where it landed between Katie and Nell Ingram, a young brunette from down the street. Nell yelped and brought up her hands to protect herself, but Katie Stuart merely sat there, carelessly lounging in her mourning clothing. She rarely wore a corset or a girdle.

"Heavily fact-checked, did you say? Catherine Belle arrived in Charleston in 1717, and that's just one of several errors."

Katie let out a breath of smoke, then bent over and snubbed out her cigarette in the coffee table ashtray. "Pierre Belle and his son, Denis, arrived in 1717. Catherine and Nelie arrived the following year."

She gestured at the magazine. "Like the article says, the whole family was supposed to take the underground railroad to Switzerland, then on to London, where they would sail for the New World. Unfortunately, Catherine and Nelie were the only two family members to survive."

"The underground railroad?" Nell Ingram picked up the magazine.

"Wherever people are oppressed, underground railroads flourish."

Nell had not read the article since all magazine subscriptions, even the newspaper, had been canceled by her father after the collapse of the market. And she did not read the article now. When Rachel pointed at the copy of *Vanity Fair*, Nell dropped the magazine like it was a hot potato.

"You insinuate that our family began in Charleston as merchants. I don't remember anyone in the Belle family being a shopkeeper—ever! It would be beneath us. The Belles were from Paris!"

Katie opened her mouth, then closed it.

Hartleigh stopped her knitting. What was going on here? If Katie Stuart got her facts wrong, the *Piedmont* would've shown her the door. Instead, almost every year, she won awards for her reporting. What was she not telling? What was she not telling Rachel?

"And you wrote that our family was not welcome in the best circles of Charleston. We were one of the best families. We are one of the best families in Charleston."

Nervous glances flashed between Nell, Sue Ellen, and Hartleigh. Hartleigh dropped the booties and her needles into her knitting bag beside her chair. This pair was blue, but she had also knitted a pink pair in secret.

"And to say that Catherine Belle dealt with pirates or red Indians—that would've been so common."

"Rachel," said Hartleigh, "should you be out of bed?"

"She's slandered my family . . . and . . . and what's worse, she's a member of my family. I really don't know how you sleep at night, Katie."

"Sue Ellen," ordered Hartleigh, "please get a chair for Rachel."

The pregnant woman held up a hand. "I don't need a chair. I'm going back upstairs."

"Not without sitting down for a moment, you aren't." Again Hartleigh gestured at Sue Ellen to get the chair.

The pregnant woman stomped her foot. "I'm telling you, I don't need to sit down."

Katie sat up. "Please sit down, Rachel."

"Yes, yes," said Nell, half rising off the loveseat,

"you don't want to deliver in the middle of the parlor."

"I won't . . ." She waved away the objection, and the girls thought Rachel just might swoon. "I won't . . ."

Sue Ellen scooted the chair under Rachel, who immediately sat down.

"Nell," said Hartleigh, "please pour a little bit of sherry."

"I'll get it!"

Katie went over to the dry bar behind the Queen Anne chairs, poured a small amount of sherry into a thimble-sized glass, and returned to Rachel where she held the small glass so the distraught woman could sip the sherry.

When she finished, Rachel nodded. "Thank you."

"Think nothing of it."

At the bar, Katie downed a glass of her own. In her many interviews, she had had more than her share of confrontations, but not with a woman so close to delivering.

"But why didn't you come to me?" asked Rachel once Katie had returned to the loveseat.

"You were in Wisconsin, and if I'd told you what I was doing, there would have been all this back and forth with long distance charges. Really, I didn't think any farmer in Wisconsin subscribed to *Vanity Fair*, and when you returned home to have your babies, you could scold me then. Who knew you'd wait this long to come home."

"So you felt you could write all these lies with impunity?"

"It was an opportunity for a girl from Greenville, South Carolina, to write for *Vanity Fair*. Yankees love stories about the South."

"But why didn't you speak to my father or my

mother? At least you wouldn't have misspelled Denis Belle's name."

"The spellings came straight from Catherine's diary."

"What?" Rachel straightened up. "What diary?"

Again the other girls perked up.

"For as long as I've been coming to Charleston, I've heard stories about one of the Belle girls marrying a pirate. I asked your father about it. He was down in the dumps after the Panic and let it slip that if the story were true it would be in Catherine's diary. I found her diary in one of trunks up in the attic. Seemed like an odd place to keep an important piece of Charleston history."

"I've never heard of this diary," said Rachel.

"Why should you?" Sue Ellen laughed. "Southern families have their own way of relating their history."

"And it's much easier to believe family myths than to do the research," added Katie.

"Well," said Nell, "our families do appear more heroic when a family member tells those tales. I was in junior high before I realized the South had lost the Civil War."

"War Between the States," corrected Sue Ellen.

"No, no, the War of Northern Aggression," suggested Hartleigh.

"More revisionist history," said Katie, shaking her head. "In Charleston, it was called the Civil War."

"But I've never heard it called the Civil War unless some Yankee called it that," said Nell.

"I learned that by reading Jennie Belle's diary. In case you're interested, Jennie's diaries of her war years are in the library at Cooper Hill. Jennie is the Belle who saved Cooper Hill from Sherman by reminding the general that her cousin, Franklin, was serving on Grant's staff."

"I thought Lewis Belle did that," said Sue Ellen, "you know, after the war."

"Not at all," said Katie, "and *Vanity Fair* wants that story, too. I've always thought the women of this family are much more important than we've been led to believe."

"Women generally are," said Hartleigh, smiling. "We just can't let on to the menfolk."

Everyone except Rachel laughed. "I thought Pierre Belle resettled the Belles in Charleston in 1717."

"True, but his niece, Catherine, made it work."

"Wait," said Nell, picking up the magazine again, "then who was Denis Belle?"

"Pierre's son."

"Catherine married her cousin?"

"Yes."

"Ugh!"

"Eeeeew!"

"Aw, come on, girls, so that the Belle name would live on in the New World. It wasn't all that uncommon."

"Still," started Nell. "Marrying your cousin . . ."

The room went silent as the girls considered the number of fools in their extended family.

"That's unreal," said one of them.

"Stupid," said another.

"Gross."

Everyone looked at Nell.

"Gross?" they asked.

"I heard it on the radio." That is, thought Nell, before the radio was repossessed. She had pleaded in vain with her father to continue the time payments, but he had said they must economize. His actions rattled Nell. How could her father be so worried about money when he owned so many grocery stores?

"If Catherine had married outside the family," explained Katie, "all her father's efforts to begin anew in America would've been lost. Pierre and his son, Denis, were pretty much wastrels, so it was up to Catherine to keep the wolf from the door."

"Well," said Nell, "all she had to do was marry another Huguenot."

"No. Catherine was a Belle and felt that she must, at all costs, preserve the family line."

Rachel nodded. "I can understand that."

"You're all snobs," said Sue Ellen, taking her Lucky Strikes from a black clutch purse, "worried about what people think, and if you have the proper surnames."

"Well, of course," said Nell, laughing. "Charleston *is* the center of the universe."

"Sue Ellen," said Hartleigh, "that's the pot calling the kettle black. If you didn't think Charleston was so special, you'd be living in New York right now."

Rachel shivered, remembering the two men who had tried to stop their car on that dark, lonely road in Wisconsin. "Well, I've had enough of living up north." To explain her shivers, she quickly added, "It's awfully cold up there." Thankfully, she would never see those men again.

"I, for one," said Hartleigh, "could stand another trip to New York City." As a belated honeymoon, James had taken his bride to New York for dining, dancing, and a few Broadway shows. Hartleigh had loved it. Window shopping on Fifth Avenue was another world.

"Really?" Sue Ellen waved out her match and tossing it in the ashtray. "A trip to New York is supposed to take my mind off losing my baby?" She offered the pack to Katie, shaking out the loose cigarettes so her cousin-in-law could select one.

Katie took a cigarette and tapped it on the back of her hand. "What I think Hartleigh is saying is that she thinks you might find another baby in New York."

"That's where I got my baby." Hartleigh's hand rose to her mouth. "On a train ride to New York."

"Oh, yeah," said Sue Ellen, "a woman traveling alone. That'll be the day."

Katie lit the cigarette, waved out the match, and gestured at the girl beside her. "Then take Nell along."

Nell's head jerked up from *Vanity Fair*. "What?"

"Wouldn't you like to go to New York?" asked Katie.

"Of course, but Daddy says we must economize."

"James will pay for it," said Hartleigh.

"Oh, I couldn't let you do that."

Letting out a smoke-filled breath, Sue Ellen said, "You're pretty free with my brother's money."

"I'm a Stuart now, and Stuarts don't apologize for taking what we want."

All the girls laughed, including Sue Ellen.

Nell had never been to New York, but many of her friends had, especially during the Twenties when flappers made New York sound like *it* was the center of the universe.

"And best of all," said Katie, "Nell will meet a good number of eligible young men."

"Oh, yes," said Rachel, smiling. "The bloom is off the rose with my marriage to a boy from Wisconsin."

"Yes," agreed Hartleigh, "we must get this old maid married and soon."

"How old are you, Nell?" asked Katie.

"Twenty-five."

"Oh, yes," said Rachel, "we must get this girl married before she sees another birthday."

Katie leaned back on the loveseat and blew a couple of smoke rings. "Nell, if you don't mind me asking, how did you miss out on marrying one of the boys who came here to build the bridge?"

Nell shrugged. "Just my bad luck, I imagine."

And a father who hovered over the family, making all their decisions. Last year, no young man had been good enough for his daughter, but now, after the Panic, it would appear that any young man would do. And when her father wasn't promoting one suitor over another, he wandered the house babbling about the collapse of RCA, one of the real high flyers.

Rachel asked, "Isn't Nicholas Eaton rooming with your husband in New York?"

Sue Ellen nodded.

Nicholas Eaton was a graduate of MIT and one of the young men who had come south to build the bridge. Nell thought she and Nick had hit it off, but then, a long lost fiancée that Nick failed to mention arrived from New England and Nell had seen Nick for what he was: a playboy.

"I'd still have to have Daddy's permission." Well, good luck, thought Nell. Her father spent evenings in his study worrying about whether he could meet the family's financial obligations. Even her mother had stopped blaming her graying hair on Nell's matrimonial state. Now she blamed a lack of money for running a proper household.

"What next?" her mother had asked. Would they have to let the help go? Would she and Nell have to do all the cooking and cleaning? If so, how appealing would that make her daughter with broken nails and red, raw hands?

Oh, why hadn't Nell married during the days of easy money and easier credit? Nowadays, if a young man had money, he sat on his wallet—and his parents sat on him.

She'd missed her chance with the boys who had come to town to build the bridge, instead, choosing to go dancing with a different fellow almost every night and relishing the fact that her father made it easy to play hard-to-get.

It might not be obvious to those who visited Charleston, but the world had changed, and Nell Ingram just might need a proper hero, a steadfast suitor who would stand by her as the world went to hell in a handbasket.

TWELVE

A knock at the front door only reinforced Nell's sense of uneasiness and she had to remind herself that no one was coming here to repossess anything in this house. James and Hartleigh had money. Rachel and Christian had money. Even Sue Ellen and Katie had money.

It was true that her family owned a series of grocery stores across the low country and as far north as the midlands. And the business had been steadily growing until the Panic hit. Now, according to her father, two stores stood unfinished, and three others, marginal stores, had been closed.

It made no sense to Nell. People still had to eat. They did, agreed her father, but since the Panic, people ate what could be bartered for or could be fished from the sea. These days grocery stores competed, not only for customers, but for product from farmers and fishermen. Competing with your suppliers wasn't something you worried about when everyone was riding high.

Not standing on ceremony, Katie answered the front door and returned with the sheriff of Charleston County.

Hat in hand, the sheriff asked, "Which one of you is Mrs. Randolph?"

Everyone in the parlor looked at Hartleigh.

"I'm Hartleigh Randolph Stuart. My mother is Elizabeth Randolph, but she's not here. What's this all about?"

"I'm sorry for your loss."

"Thank you." Hartleigh realized everyone in the parlor still wore black.

"I'm looking for a runaway girl. Her name is Dory Campbell." He looked from one young woman to the other. "I was told she lived here."

"I don't think—"

"Sue Ellen," cut in Hartleigh, "She's the girl who hung around while the bridge was being built."

Everyone nodded with the exception of Katie, who'd never met the girl.

"Also known as the 'brat,'" injected Rachel.

"Rachel, that's rather harsh, don't you think?"

"Is she still here?" asked the sheriff.

"No."

"Good riddance."

"Please, Rachel . . ."

"She did leave rather abruptly. You must give me that."

Hartleigh nodded. She didn't know what to say, but she would not betray her mother.

"I hope you counted the silver," said Rachel.

Hartleigh said, "One day Dory was here, then she was gone." That wasn't a lie.

"Who did she leave with?"

The girls looked at each other.

"Leave with?" asked Hartleigh.

"Did she leave in a taxi?" The sheriff knew Elizabeth Randolph had left in a taxi from this very house less than a year ago.

Hartleigh didn't know what to say. She looked at the others, but no help there. "We don't have a car, so occasionally we use a taxi service."

Sue Ellen brightened. "I live next door. The Randolphs can use our car."

"Or my family's car," said Rachel.

The sheriff hated interviewing women. Their conversation went everywhere and nowhere.

"Did you notify the authorities?"

"Oh, you mean like the Orphan House? No."

"I'm opposed to that," said Rachel. "We need to move the children living in the Orphan House into foster homes."

"So no one knows where she went?" asked the sheriff, looking from one girl to the other.

All shook their heads but Katie.

She said, "Sorry, but I can't help you. I'm just in town for the funeral." Then, feeling the sense of apprehension in the room, Katie quickly added, "But the idea of a runaway girl leaving by taxi sounds rather far-fetched."

"Well, thank you, ladies," said the sheriff, gesturing with his hat at Rachel. "And you may wish to check your silverware as the young lady suggested. Dory's family reported several billfolds being emptied before she left their farm near Summerville."

"And the family has just begun searching for her now?" asked Katie.

"We just received a report of Dory being seen in this neighborhood."

"Well, she's gone now," said Sue Ellen, nodding.

"Thank you again, ladies."

Katie followed the sheriff to the door.

"I told you that girl was trouble," said Rachel, lowering her voice.

"I didn't even know her last name," said Sue Ellen.

"Well, you certainly cozied up to her fast enough. You even took her sailing."

"She had serious problems at home, but she wouldn't talk about them."

"You've had serious problems at home and you've never talked about them. The difference is that one day that girl was here and then she was gone."

Showing the sheriff out, Katie saw a rawboned man and his son standing on the front porch, hats in hands. At the curb stood a Charleston police officer, probably assigned to escort the sheriff around the jurisdiction of the CPD. Both the older and young man wore their Sunday best. Being the good reporter, Katie left the door cracked to hear more.

The sheriff explained what he had been told.

"They're lying," said the boy. "I saw her run into this house."

"Well," said the sheriff, "maybe you'll want to talk to a solicitor. There's a young one by the name of Billy Ray Craven who's itching to make a name for himself."

They didn't need this hassle, thought Katie, not when their family was the largest bootlegger in the state. She opened the door and stepped out on the porch. She introduced herself again, adding that she was from the upstate.

"Occasionally, my friends mention Dory."

"See, Pa, I tole you."

"What I know is very elementary. When she was hungry, Dory worked in the kitchen and did odd jobs. On occasion, she was allowed to sleep in the carriage house with the other servants."

"She slept with the Negroes?" asked the older man. The only servants working in Charleston were Negroes.

"What's your interest in this, sir?" asked Katie.

"She's my daughter."

"She's my sister," said the boy, "and I swore I'd protect her."

The father looked at his son with some degree of hostility.

"Well," said Katie to the sheriff, "finding her could be a problem. I understand she was a real will-o'-the-wisp."

"Dory was no ghost," said the brother. "She was a real person."

Katie ignored the brother and spoke to the sheriff. "It's a rather delicate matter that I don't care to discuss in mixed company."

"Perhaps there's a male in the household I could speak with," offered the sheriff.

"This is James Stuart's house. He runs Stuart and Company."

"I know the man." The sheriff didn't want to talk with Stuart either. It might upset *their* delicate relationship.

"Perhaps you could stop by the warehouse."

"We'll do that," said the sheriff, tipping his hat to Katie, "and if you don't mind, would you call ahead and tell Captain Stuart to wait for us at the warehouse if he's planning on leaving?"

"Yes, of course."

"He could leave before we get there," muttered the brother as he followed his father and the sheriff down the steps.

"Captain Stuart's an honorable man. He'll do the right thing."

The three of them rejoined the beat cop on the sidewalk. While the Campbells climbed into the sheriff's patrol car, the beat cop was taken aside and asked several questions by the sheriff. Once or twice the two law enforcement officers glanced in the direction of the house.

That was enough for Katie. She quickly returned to the house and dialed the number of the warehouse.

When connected to James, she brought him up to date. "See if you can sidestep the issue of who Dory left town with. That seems to be of particular interest to the sheriff."

"Will do." What irony, thought James. Now it was his job to protect the one woman in the world who truly despised him.

James hung up the phone. "The county sheriff is dropping by."

Everyone looked apprehensive. Several looked for a way out of the building.

"No, no, no. Nothing to worry about. Alexander, back one of the trucks outside and raise the hood. Take some tools with you and lay out a cloth to protect the paint job. Roddey, take a smoke break. When the sheriff arrives, come in and tell me. No one wants to see the inside of this warehouse, especially the sheriff."

When James was called outside, he joined the sheriff and a Deputy Bumgarner who patrolled the area around the Campbell family farm. The deputy carried a shotgun over his shoulder.

Ordering the Campbells to remain in the patrol car, the three men gathered at the hood of the truck where Alexander was working on the engine. Shaking hands with both law enforcement officers, James palmed the sheriff a hundred dollars and ten for the deputy.

Alexander wiped his hands on a rag. "How about some coffee for you gentlemen?"

"Good idea."

"Yeah."

"Thank you."

The Negro disappeared inside the warehouse.

"What have we got here, Stuart?" asked the sheriff.

"A runaway girl who worked in my house, off and on, for a few months. She did occasional odd jobs. My wife and her friends gave her clothing and makeup tips."

"Where did she sleep?"

"I don't know if you're aware of the showers I had installed in the old kitchen, but occasionally one of the engineers would find her sleeping there." In the past, Charleston law required all kitchens to be in a separate building to isolate any fires.

The sheriff nodded. "That sounds about right. What about Katie Stuart?"

"She married my cousin. She's a reporter for the *Piedmont*."

"She didn't remember meeting Dory."

James took out a cheroot and lit it. "I don't

think she did. Before the bridge was completed, Dory disappeared, but none of the ladies seemed particularly alarmed."

At the mention of the bridge the sheriff smiled. Everyone had an opinion about the new bridge. "This was the first winter the snowbirds could pass through Charleston headed for Florida, but they didn't come. You've ruined a beautiful harbor with that monstrosity."

After letting out a smoke-filled breath, James explained. "We're just waiting for the economy to turn around."

Another smile from the sheriff. "Can you put a date on that?" No new deputies had been hired since the Panic and the criminal element seemed to know it.

James shook his head.

"Granddaddy says the American economy always comes back," said the deputy with the shotgun over his shoulder. "It did in '21, '07, and the worst of the lot, 1893."

"And every time the rich got richer," groused the sheriff.

Stuart had his own question. "Does your deputy have to carry that shotgun?"

"Bumgarner, why *are* you carrying that shotgun?"

"Sorry." The deputy appeared chagrined. "I just thought this was a raid."

The sheriff snorted. "Raid Stuart and Company? Then how would you afford all those knickknacks for your girlfriend? Get rid of the shotgun. Lock it in the trunk of your patrol car."

"Yes, sir."

James puffed on his cheroot as the deputy walked

away. "Dory told my sister that she wanted to travel the world. I wouldn't be surprised if the girls gave her some walking-around money."

"That sounds dangerous, a girl wandering around alone."

"Dory knew how to wrap her chest like all the other girls. She could pass for a boy if she had to."

"So it's unlikely we'll find her in some shallow grave in the Francis Marion Reservation?"

"Doubt it." James stared at the patrol car where the Campbells sat. "My wife always suspected that Dory was mistreated at home."

The deputy returned.

"Bumgarner," asked the sheriff, "you heard any stories about the Campbells?"

The deputy shrugged. "It must've have been a passel of work for a girl with a father and three brothers. Dory was a small thing. I don't blame her for running off."

"But why come home now?" asked the sheriff.

The deputy didn't understand the question.

"Look at it this way. Why is it okay for Dory to return home now, but not a year ago or even six months ago?" The sheriff glanced at the patrol car himself. "What's happened in that family? What's new? What's different?"

The deputy considered the question as Alexander returned with mugs of steaming coffee.

"Thank you, Alexander."

"Yeah," said the sheriff.

"Got any sugar?" asked the deputy.

In a moment, Alexander returned with a sugar bowl and several spoons. Deputy Bumgarner dumped in a good bit of sugar and cream.

"Good coffee," said the sheriff, drinking his black.

"Thank you, sir." Alexander returned to the warehouse.

After a long pull off his coffee, the deputy said, "Campbell's wife died a couple of years ago. Then their oldest son signed up for the navy, and as far as I know he's never come home. Told his friends he was going to be a lifer, and that's thirty years or more."

"When did he go in?"

"Summer of '28, if I remember correctly."

"So the eldest son wasn't around for the fall harvest?"

"And shortly after he left, Dory shows up at my place," added James.

"And Campbell is left with two sons to run the family farm. And no one to cook or clean."

Bumgarner snapped his fingers. "No, he's not! Campbell remarried. Real young thing."

The sheriff made a face. "I'm getting a bad feeling about this. How long ago did Campbell remarry?"

"Oh, a month ago or so."

"And now," said James, "the brother thinks it's safe for Dory to return home and comes looking for his sister."

The sheriff shook his head. "Dory not only cleaned and cooked, but took her mother's place in bed."

"And before she was twelve," added James.

"Happens all the time. Daddy doesn't have time for courting."

"Well," said Bumgarner, "these are hard times."

"How old's the bride?" asked James of the deputy.

"Does it matter?" asked the sheriff.

"So what do we do?" asked his deputy.

"The boy needs to know his sister's safe," said the

sheriff. He sipped from his coffee. "It's probably all he thinks about. Daddy came along to keep an eye on the boy. Not that I have any jurisdiction over child brides."

"Tell them you'll look into it," said James. "I'll see what I can come up with."

"Well, good luck, but I don't think any man's been married long enough to discuss this with his wife." To the deputy: "Take the Campbells home. And watch what you say. I'll want to speak to them before you leave."

The deputy threw away the remaining coffee and left the mug on the hood of the truck.

Once Bumgarner left, the sheriff said, "Stuart, you need to locate your mother-in-law and have her return that girl to Charleston. If that boy could find your house—"

"Dory and the brother probably had a secret meeting place, or at least a hollowed-out tree where they left messages."

"It could've been easier than Tom Sawyer," said the sheriff. "While the bridge was going up, people by the hundreds strolled along the shore of the Cooper, especially on Sundays."

James glanced at the patrol car. "What will you tell the Campbells?"

The sheriff grinned before walking away. "That I've got my best man on the case."

THIRTEEN

Inside, James met with the collectors, the men who picked up the money from the various accounts. Most were large, beefy, and no-nonsense. James explained that he had turned over the bordellos to Petrocelli and that Stuart and Company would no longer deal in dope. There was some grousing from a few, many disbelieving.

"Hey, you want to go to work for Petrocelli? That's fine with me." James pulled out a wad of cash. "Here's a hundred dollars for anyone who wants to turn in his book and cash."

Two men stepped forward, one who had found Jesus and another who had gambling debts up to his eyeballs.

"Lewis, please debrief these men and relieve them of their notebooks."

The two former collectors were taking notebooks and envelopes from their pockets as they left the warehouse office.

"Christian," asked James, "would you see them off the property?"

Christian followed the three men out the office door.

"What'd the sheriff want?" asked one of the collectors.

"What do the cops usually want?" said Prescott from his wheelchair. "More money."

"Let's not get off track here," said James. "I'm sure those two won't be the last to leave. Everyone has his own management style. Just remember, one hundred dollars is waiting for anyone who leaves. Roddey, I believe you want to introduce your cousins who've come to work in the warehouse."

Roddey did.

Again James addressed the group. "I want to thank all of you for honoring my father by attending the funeral. There will be an extra ten in your paycheck this week."

Next, he introduced Prescott Mitchell as the new office manager, explaining that Roddey's mother had retired. One of Roddey's cousins made a face. If James noticed, he ignored it.

"Christian Andersen will be the assistant manager. There's entirely too much liquor in this place, so it's evident that Roddey needs some help. That's why I hired Prescott—to keep Roddey and Christian out of the office and on the warehouse floor. When you think about it, this whole warehouse is a drag on profits. For this reason, we will soon begin meeting the rumrunners with a fleet of trucks right at the beach. From there, the booze will travel inland, straight to our customers."

"Does that mean a raise?" asked one of the sour-faced collectors who leaned against the low railing.

"I kind of thought you might accept divvying up the accounts of the departing bagmen."

There was a general nodding of heads and verbal affirmations.

James put his hands on Prescott's shoulders. "Now, Mister Mitchell will explain how the warehouse will operate."

From his wheelchair, Prescott said, "Captain Stuart was the site engineer for the bridge project. What this means is that about a month from now he will know everything about this operation, and if you don't produce, you'll be gone."

Prescott glanced up at James. "That means me, too. I know I'm a cripple, but Captain Stuart appreciates my capabilities." Prescott went on to detail how he would run the office based on what he had been told by both Roddey and Lewis Belle.

Returning to the office with Lewis, Christian said, "Captain Stuart, those off-duty policemen you had the chief send over are here for their assignments."

"Very good. Roddey, you set their shifts so at least one man is on duty at all times and two men at night."

Roddey nodded, picked up his clipboard, and went out the door.

"Now," said Prescott Mitchell, clapping his hands together, "let's move some hooch!"

Lewis divided the accounts among the current staff. There were arguments about one or two, but on the whole they spread the wealth around. Prescott was left to attend to the details while James put his arm on Lewis's shoulder and took the attorney aside.

"I know this is not going to make any sense to you, but I don't want anything to do with cheap whiskey."

Lewis pulled away. "What are you saying?"

James tugged the older man back into him. "I'm saying if Samuel Chase wants that business, I'll sell it to him, but I must have another name on that operation, not Stuart and Company."

"That's crazy. There's too much money to be made in watered-down hooch."

"Lewis, just be a good friend and find a way to get Stuart and Company out of the cheap liquor business."

"Cousin Jimmy and Jeb aren't going to like this."

"Sorry, but in the long line of Stuarts who have run this company, none of them would've wanted the family selling a shoddy product."

"James, your ancestor was a pirate."

"And your family started out as shopkeepers. Both families rose above their circumstances by performing quality work."

Lewis opened his mouth to object, then closed his mouth and closed his eyes. After a long sigh, he opened them again. "You know this could mean the end to Stuart and Company."

"I beg to disagree. There'll always be a demand for good liquor and Stuart and Company will always provide it." James clapped his friend on the shoulder. "By the way, why aren't we invested in textiles? Cousin Jimmy has a share in one of those mills in Greenville. Why not us? Why not buy a whole mill? God knows there's plenty of money lying around to do it.

"Uh-huh. I know the answer. Jimmy likes the big money that comes from bootlegging. All of you are addicted to it, and you're going to miss it when Prohibition ends."

"James, I don't want to go round and round again about this pipe dream of yours."

"Well, then," said James, smiling, "I'll drop the subject if you won't forget it." He stuffed his notepad inside his coat pocket and put away his fountain pen. "Now, let's make the rounds. You know, Petrocelli, the gin mill, and the little man in the cage."

"That's going to make for a very long night."

Pulling him close again, James lowered his voice. "Did I ever tell you the secret of successful management?"

"No. I don't believe you did."

"While building the Cooper River Bridge, I would show up anywhere, anytime, you know, just wander around all day."

"And in your wandering, who did you wear out last time?"

"Alexander."

"Did his wife complain?"

"Why, yes, matter of fact, she did."

Lewis sighed. "As has my wife."

That night, James stumbled over someone as he came through the gate at front of his house.

"What the devil?" He dropped his cheroot and went to his hands and knees over the figure.

When the kid tried to slip away, James caught one of his feet. "Not so fast, Benjamin."

"Get off me!"

Not Benjamin.

James grabbed the wrought-iron gate with one hand, the boy's collar with the other, and they stood up smartly. "Upsy-daisy!"

A flashlight beam hit them in the face. Benjamin had wandered over from the house next door.

"Who's that?" asked the little black boy.

James held his hand up. "Could you kill the light?" The other hand held Dory's brother. "I thought you and your father were told to go home."

"I ran away. I thought you might help me like you did Dory."

"I had nothing to do with that. I was building the bridge." He released his hold on the boy's collar.

"Well, I can't go home."

"Why's that?" asked Benjamin.

"Papa will give me another whipping."

"As he should," said James. "You disobeyed him."

The boy stared at his feet. "I've already been whipped once today because of why we came to town."

James looked from the white boy to the black one. "Benjamin, why don't you call it a night?"

"You don't want me to watch next door?"

"Not tonight. Scram!"

The boy flicked on the light and scampered around the side of the house, heading for the carriage house.

"In my car, boy."

"The name's Carl and I ain't going home."

"I'm not taking you home. I'm taking you somewhere you'll be safe for the night, and I don't want to hear another yip out of you."

Hartleigh was reading *All Quiet on the Western Front* when James came in. A talkie had been made from the novel, and she couldn't wait to see it. In the background, an RCA Radiola played music from the NBC radio network, a gift from her husband to keep his wife from going stir-crazy.

Hartleigh glanced at the clock. "James, goodness, it's almost midnight."

"Long day at the office."

"You're not getting enough sleep and you're never here for meals."

"I always eat breakfast with Mother."

"And you're a good son for doing that, but I don't see you until late at night. At least Christian comes home for our luncheon and Rachel can monitor his meals."

James took off his coat and hung it in an armoire. "Christian's not the boss." He sat down to take off his shoes.

"Well, your being the boss is preventing you from having a regular life. You are regular, aren't you?"

James stopped unlacing a shoe and looked up. "I can't believe you asked me that question."

"I'm your wife, James. I'm responsible for your well-being."

Returning to his shoes, he said, "I'm not going to discuss it."

"Fine, but if you won't come home at a decent hour, you're going to have to take a spoonful of castor oil every night." She gestured at the dresser. "The spoon and bottle are over there."

James straightened up and looked at the dresser. "Is this some kind of a gag?"

"I've asked you to see Doctor Rose when he's here, but you're never here. Rose recommends a daily dose of castor oil just to be safe."

"But I'm not . . . I'm not . . . Hartleigh, I'm not going to take that medicine. It's for children." He removed the last shoe.

"James, you must take care of yourself so that you can take care of me and the baby. You can't do that if you're down with a cold, the flu, or distracted by a flare up of irregularity."

James stared at his wife, especially her sizable belly, then got to his feet and went over to the dresser. There he made a face after swallowing a spoonful of castor oil, shivering at the taste. He wiped the spoon clean and put it aside. He'd never liked the stuff.

When he pulled on his robe to go to the bathroom, Hartleigh said, "Darling, there's something I wish to ask you."

Now what?

"Did the sheriff come by the warehouse this afternoon?"

"He did." James stepped from behind a dressing screen.

"And?"

"He put me in charge of not only finding Dory but returning her safely to Charleston."

"He didn't!"

"He did."

Hartleigh's eyes widened, and then she began to laugh.

Cinching his robe tight, James said, "I'm pleased I could cheer you up."

His comment made his wife laugh even harder.

James went to the bathroom, but when he returned, his wife was still giggling, hiding her mouth behind her hand. James growled and turned in for the night.

Hartleigh knew newlyweds weren't supposed to go to bed mad, but she wasn't mad. She was laughing. Considering the strained relationship between her mother and her husband, it was the funniest thing she'd heard lately. Tears ran down her cheeks as she made a note on the pad on the nightstand. She turned out the light, still giggling.

Before she knew it, her husband was out of bed and pulling on his robe again. "I think I'll sleep downstairs."

Hartleigh wanted to call out "No! No! No!" but when her husband left, she could only snicker.

The moment James walked into the warehouse the following morning, the phone rang.

"It's for you," said Prescott. "He's called several times."

Puzzled, James picked up the phone on the table. It was the sheriff.

"What am I supposed to do with this kid, Stuart?"

"I couldn't send him home. He's in fear for his life."

"It's none of our business what goes on in that family."

"A man in uniform speaks with more authority than a liquor distributor."

The sheriff laughed, then paused. "Wait a darn minute, that gives me an idea. Campbell's brother owns property next to his, and where Campbell's a teetotaler, his brother isn't."

"Meaning?"

"If Campbell beats his son again, we give his brother to the revenuers. The brother has a still."

"You think that's enough?"

"Oh, yeah, that'll work. Remember Campbell's new bride? Bumgarner told me the girl is actually his brother's daughter, if you can believe that."

"Campbell married his niece?"

"What can I say? He likes them young. According to Bumgarner, Campbell's first wife was a child bride."

"But, seriously now, aren't you on the brother's payroll?"

"For ten dollars a month."

"And you have no reservations about turning him in to the revenuers?"

"None whatsoever. Drinking comes natural to a man, but selling family members into white slavery is quite another matter."

Later that morning, Prescott rolled over in his chair and handed the phone to James. "It's Cousin Jimmy."

When James answered, Jimmy asked, "Who's that?"

"Prescott Mitchell."

"The happy-go-lucky guy who fell off the bridge?"

"The same."

"Boy, you sure know how to pick them."

"Is Luke Andersen on his way back to Charleston?"

"Be there this afternoon. I've got Jolly driving the other truck. But that's not why I called." And Jimmy gave James a piece of his mind about giving away Stuart and Company's brothels.

James waited for his cousin to run down. "Are you invested in any cathouses in the upstate?" he asked.

"Of course not. Katie would kill me."

"Well, I have one of those at home, too."

"Jeb isn't going to like this."

"Jeb's a sailor. As long as he has access to a bordello, he'll be just fine and dandy."

"I don't know . . ."

"You also believe in selling dope when hardly anyone in the Carolinas uses dope."

"Still, there's a demand."

"For a product that creates customers who're out of their mind or so languid they can't hold down a job. Now, I have a question for you."

"I'm listening."

"Why isn't Stuart and Company in textiles? There's a business that'll last much longer than Prohibition."

Next his broker called.

"Sorry to hear about your father, James, but have I got a deal for you. We're selling shares in fixed investment trusts, and all the slots will be sold, first come, first serve."

"Pray tell," asked James, "what kind of gimmick is that?"

"No gimmicks. The shares you purchase are the absolute best stocks the market has to offer."

"Thirty billion dollars vanishes in four days and you think there are still some good stocks left?"

"President Hoover said such an adjustment was necessary and the Fed says we're through the worst of it."

When James said nothing, his broker went on. "Chase Bank just bought two of its competitors. You think those smart Yankee boys would be buying if they thought they should be selling?"

"I don't know. I've been tied up lately and haven't had time to consider it. I'll be in touch."

"No, sirree. I have daughters. I'll be in touch with you."

Next, Hartleigh called. "I missed you this morning, darling."

"You were asleep. I didn't want to wake you."

"You're very sweet, James. I called to apologize about my giggling fit. I couldn't help it."

"I could see your point, given your mother's low regard for me."

"If I could reach Momma by phone . . ."

"Please don't. Send a wire. We need Dory returned to Charleston to put out this fire. The government could accuse your mother of . . ."

"What?"

"Have you ever heard . . . I'm really not comfortable discussing this with—"

"James, I'm your wife. We have a completely different relationship now that we're wed."

"As I've noticed . . ."

"James, would you stop pussyfooting around the issue."

"Have you ever heard of the Mann Act?"

Evidently his wife had. "My mother kidnapped no one!"

"Dory is under the age of consent, my dear."

"And I should be concerned with that? Are you planning on ratting out my mother?"

And from there the conversation went downhill.

FOURTEEN

Before her wife-beating father fell into the Ashley and drowned, Sue Ellen's movements had been severely restricted by her brother and his wife, who always had her best interests at heart.

Sue Ellen wasn't interested in what was best for her, only what she enjoyed the most, and that turned out to be a physical relationship with a man. As for the servants playing the rat, the Stuarts had always been known to overpay and to have a lenient policy when it came to days off. The servants would be no problem as long as she was discreet.

But two weeks before her father died, Sue Ellen learned she was pregnant. And she hadn't been with her husband in several months, yet she intuitively knew to play hard to get when Hartleigh suggested that she and Nell Ingram travel to New York. Sue Ellen cursed her luck. Neighbors expected her to be here for her mother, a ghostly presence who drifted through the house.

Which brought to mind the clinic. The clinic had been started by the good women of Charleston as a place for girls to dispose of unwanted pregnancies. Dr. Rose stopped by once a week to perform the procedures, and the clinic had been so successful that Rose now spent another half day there.

This was not what the benevolent matrons of Charleston had expected for their generosity. Dr. Rose should be making house calls south of Broad instead of traveling west of the Ashley. Now Sue Ellen would have to cross the Ashley, her own personal Rubicon, but only if someone accompanied her.

Queen-of-France Rachel was out of the question; Katie could fly off in a moment's notice; and because Hartleigh had good days and bad days, she couldn't count on her. Dr. Rose had become more and more concerned that Hartleigh could only deliver by Caesarian. So Sue Ellen set her sights on Nell Ingram.

At the visitation, she had asked Nell and Franklin to remain behind, and while the Stuart men gathered in her father's study to discuss the future of Stuart and Company, Sue Ellen asked Nell and Franklin to escort Hartleigh home. From there it was a short stroll up South Battery to the Ingrams' house.

Later, she learned that during the walk home, all Franklin could talk about was his overbearing stepmother.

"She wants me to court girls from Savannah and Augusta," complained Franklin, as he walked along, swinging his cane. "All that time wasted driving back and forth to Savannah or Augusta." He shook his head.

Nell had grown up with Franklin, so she knew the suggestion by his stepmother was a nonstarter.

Franklin would never reach Savannah. He'd make too many stops along the way.

Walking Nell to her front porch, Franklin asked, "Why do you think we're the last two in our circle to still be single?"

Nell said she could not speak for him, but the right boy had never asked her. And when Franklin started in on Georgiana again, Nell took his hand, squeezed it, and made him promise to marry for love, not because of the demands of his stepmother. She would even lend him a helping hand; then Nell stood on her tiptoes, pecked Franklin on the cheek, and disappeared inside.

Franklin stumbled down the steps unable to believe his good fortune. Nell Ingram was just the girl to help him find a wife. Nell had attended both Ashley Hall and College of Charleston and had connections in the midlands. As he turned out of the gate, twirling his cane like a baton, Franklin strutted toward home, fortified that he could meet any challenge with Nell Ingram at his side.

Nell's mother, dressed in a robe and slippers, sat in front of the fireplace, a glass of buttermilk in her hand.

"Nell," she asked, "who walked you home?"

"Franklin Belle."

"And you didn't invite him in?"

"It's late, Mother, and it's been a long day. Even you're ready for bed." Nell leaned down, gave her mother a kiss, and turned to go. "See you in the morning," she said rather cheerily.

"Darling, have you ever considered our neighbor, Franklin Belle?"

At the parlor door, Nell faced her again. "Franklin's immune to feminine charms. All he wants to do is spend time drawing plants, trees, and bushes."

"Perhaps you should accompany him."

"Mother, now how would that look?"

"You could always . . . what does your generation call it?"

"Double date?"

"Yes, yes. That would be appropriate."

Nell smiled. "I've gone with him to the woods—"

Her mother appeared to be stricken. "How dare the young man—"

"Oh, no, Mother, it was a church picnic, and all Franklin did was spend the afternoon drawing. Even Hartleigh, whom Franklin was dating at the time, finally gave up in exasperation. That's why Hartleigh ended up with James."

"Franklin's not . . . a sissy boy, is he?"

"Oh, no, Mother. It's just that girls are not the great passion of his life."

"Well, I certainly hope some girl will be able to change that."

"Many have tried, Mother. Franklin is, after all, a Belle of Charleston."

The following day, Sue Ellen pounced on Franklin when Rachel reminded her brother of their mother's birthday. Franklin usually dropped by to lunch with his sister.

"Yes," agreed Sue Ellen, nodding, "you must get your mother a gift."

"Stepmother."

"Don't be rude." Rachel handed a list of suggestions across the table to Sue Ellen. The luncheon featured chicken and broccoli casserole. "And if you wouldn't mind, I'll need something—as will my father—for Georgiana."

That caused Franklin to raise an eyebrow.

Rachel saw the look. "She's still our mother."

So when Georgiana arrived for the luncheon, Sue Ellen and Franklin went out the door with their list and Alexander trailed along to carry any packages.

In the ladies' department, Sue Ellen pointed out an especially colorful scarf. She gripped Franklin's arm. "Georgiana would absolutely love that!"

"It does have plenty of color," admitted Franklin, picking up the scarf.

"That's what makes Nell Ingram different. She doesn't force color but goes with the natural state."

"I'm sorry, but I don't think I know what you're talking about."

"Haven't you seen Nell's backyard? It's springtime, so if you dropped by, you'd see something special."

"Sue Ellen, whatever do you mean?"

"Nell is a genuine Charleston eccentric." Leaning over and whispering, she added, "Her garden is the only one south of Broad that has real plants in them."

"Er—what other kind of plants are there?"

"Oh, Franklin." Sue Ellen tried to keep the excitement out of her voice. "Nell transfers weeds from all over Charleston to the safety of her backyard. Some people take in stray cats, but with Nell, it's weeds. Think about it. Who could she tell? It's not something you brag about."

Franklin considered this and found the idea provocative. "Perhaps I should stop by and offer my encouragement. I, for one, know how difficult it is being the odd man out."

Sue Ellen nodded vigorously. "I'd make time for it. You won't believe what you'll see."

Franklin headed for the register with the scarf.

"Make sure you get it gift wrapped," she called after him.

From the cash register, Franklin nodded.

Sue Ellen lowered her voice again. "Alexander, how's Nell's garden coming along?"

"Honestly, Miss Sue Ellen, it's the worst garden I've ever seen. No boundaries, no trellises, and certainly no order. Weeds everywhere, including scrub pine. I even brought in English ivy, and that stuff grows faster than kudzu."

Sue Ellen smiled. "Kind of makes you proud, doesn't it."

"Only if Miss Nell's father doesn't shoot me next time he finds me in his backyard."

"Nell said you've collected every weed known to man."

"I'm a colored man, Miss Sue Ellen. I'm on a first-name basis with every weed in the city of Charleston."

Nell was wearing out the rug in the parlor when the doorbell rang.

Looking through the glass, Mrs. Ingram said, "Finally!"

"Mother, please!"

Her father came out of his study and strolled down the hallway. "What would really please me is to get rid of all those damn weeds in the backyard."

"Oh, no, Daddy," said Nell, shaking her head, "you can never do that."

Ingram rolled his eyes as his wife opened the door.

"Why, Franklin Belle, what are you doing here?"

"I came to see Nell's garden."

The Ingrams glanced at each other. Mr. Ingram said, "I don't know about that."

"Now, William," said his wife, "it's Nell's garden, not ours."

"You can say that again."

Mrs. Ingram shot her husband a warning look before escorting Franklin into the parlor. "Nell, darling, Franklin Belle is here."

Nell sat on the sofa with a worried look on her face. "I'm not sure about this."

"You knew this young man was paying a call?" asked her father. "When did he leave his card?"

"He didn't. Franklin called on the telephone."

"The telephone," said her father, shaking his head. "That gadget will be the ruination of civilization."

"Nell, your father and I were just going out."

"We'll be just fine, Mother."

"I don't think so."

"Your mother's right. You two should have a chaperone."

"Oh, Mister Ingram," said Franklin, grinning, "we're not going to stay inside. We'll be in Nell's garden."

"You call that monstrosity—"

"William! My coat, if you please!"

Still, it was well over fifteen minutes before Franklin could talk Nell into allowing him to see her secret garden.

Standing on the back porch the following day, Sue Ellen nodded enthusiastically. "Yes, yes, I can see why Franklin enjoyed his visit. This is truly horrible.

I do believe you owe Alexander an extra carton of cigarettes."

From one side of the yard to the other, weeds grew everywhere. The only concession to normalcy was a bird bath planted within a circle of bricks left from the building of the house over a hundred years ago. The set-aside circle was filled with begonias, bluebells, bachelor buttons, and crocus and could be seen from the kitchen window. In other parts of the backyard, azaleas, camellias, and roses fought for sunlight among weeds that proliferated everywhere. In the very rear, ajuga chocolate chip covered an area in front of Adirondack chairs badly in need of a coat of paint. Someone had run a push mower over that portion of the backyard, biting off the blue flowers of the ground covering and its flanking dandelions.

"My parents are going crazy. What will people think?"

"Don't worry, my dear" said Sue Ellen. "No one living south of Broad wants to be dropped from the Belles' Christmas list. My daddy once upset Georgiana, and I can tell you there was many a sleepless night until the invitation from the Belles arrived."

"The help might talk."

Sue Ellen took her arm. "Nell, everyone in this house has your best interest at heart. As far as your neighbors go, your backyard's like many others: you can't see their yard and they can't see yours."

"Sue Ellen, why are you doing this for me?"

"To tell the truth, I have a favor to ask of you."

To push Franklin over the top, Sue Ellen dined with Hartleigh and Rachel so she'd be there when he dropped by again. At an early supper, Franklin bubbled over about Nell's garden and what a swell girl she was. They were eating Frogmore stew, otherwise known as a low country boil, an easy one-pot seafood meal made up of corn, sausage, potatoes, and shrimp, but curiously no frogs.

Rachel glanced at Hartleigh. This was the first she'd heard any of this.

Sue Ellen jumped in with: "Franklin, you're telling secrets."

"Secrets?" asked Hartleigh.

"Have either of you seen Nell's backyard?" asked Sue Ellen, looking from brother to sister and then to her best friend sitting beside her.

"What reason would I have to go into Nell Ingram's backyard?" asked Rachel. "Doesn't her father own a bunch of supermarkets?"

"Perhaps a garden party," suggested Hartleigh.

Rachel sniffed. "I don't think so."

"Well," said Hartleigh, smiling, "something tells me you're about to get to know Nell Ingram a good deal better than you do now."

When Rachel cornered her brother in the parlor, she asked, "What's this about Nell Ingram?"

Engaged in their conversation, neither heard the front door open and close.

"I was simply enjoying the pleasure of Nell's . . ." Franklin almost said the word "weeds," but instead said, "company."

"Does Mother know?"

"Does Mother know what?" asked Georgiana, strolling into the parlor.

Franklin rose to his feet. "It's nothing, Mother."

"Franklin's sparking Nell Ingram," explained his sister from where she sat on the loveseat.

"Why wasn't I told of your intentions?"

When their stepmother took a seat on the loveseat next to his sister, Franklin sat in one of the Queen Anne chairs. "Really, Mother, I only stopped by to see her secret garden."

"Her secret garden!" asked both women at the same time.

"Yes, you see—"

"And who was your chaperone?" demanded his stepmother.

"The Ingrams were on their way out."

"On their way out!" came another dual shout.

Georgiana and Rachel looked at each other, then took each others' hands, gloves and all.

"Yes, yes," said Franklin, finally catching a glimmer of the danger lying ahead. "Nothing untoward happened."

"But there's the appearance of a lack of decorum. You had no chaperone. That girl could say anything."

"Listen to Mother, Franklin. She knows best."

"This is ridiculous. Nell's helping me find a wife."

"Helping you find a wife?"

Bewildered, Franklin said, "I don't understand. I thought you'd be pleased."

Georgiana felt weak. She just might swoon.

Rachel gripped her arm. "Are you all right?"

Georgiana put both hands beside her to remain upright on the loveseat. "I really . . . don't know."

Turning to her brother, Rachel said, "Doctor Rose is upstairs with Hartleigh. Get him immediately."

"No!" said Georgiana as her stepson rose to his feet. "Get your father. Only he can make this right."

Franklin, Senior, made a beeline for the Ingrams'. He'd been at his club when charged with the mission to get to the bottom of his son's dalliance with Nell Ingram.

Sue Ellen was coming down the front steps, and Nell was waving good-bye when the senior Franklin stormed through the wrought-iron gate. Without hesitation, both girls performed a modified curtsy.

"Mister Belle."

"Mister Belle."

"Girls." He tipped his derby to them. "Miss Ingram . . . it's Nell, isn't it?" A cute thing, thought Senior. No wonder his son had been smitten. Of course, young women wore next to nothing these days so why wouldn't a young man's blood boil when faced with such a provocative image.

"Why, yes, sir," said Nell, replying with a broad smile and a fuller curtsy. "How may I help you."

He joined Nell on the porch. "Is your father home?"

"Yes, he is. I'll announce you."

Senior held open the front door, and when Sue Ellen attempted to follow them into the house, he said, "Mrs. Hall, if we might have a moment."

"Why, of course." Sue Ellen curtsied again, then walked out to the sidewalk. And though she lingered, Nell never reappeared on the front porch.

Inside, Senior paced the parlor.

Nell appeared at the door, thoroughly shaken. "My father . . . my father asked . . . asked if you would join him in his study."

"Very well." Senior followed Nell down the hall where William Ingram stood at the door of his study.

"Mister Belle," asked Nell, "with this heat, could I

interest you in a glass of iced tea?"

"No, thank you." Senior closed the door of her father's study behind him.

Nell was joined in the hallway by her mother.

"What was that all about?"

"I have no idea."

Franklin's and Nell's fathers were not in the study long. They quickly adjourned to the backyard. Moments later, they returned to the hallway where Nell and her mother stood.

Senior took Nell's hand. "Miss Ingram, you are either the oddest young lady I've ever met or the cleverest one I've ever known. Either way, you're the perfect wife for my son." He kissed her hand and disappeared out the front door.

Nell's legs weakened, but it was her mother who swooned.

"What . . . what just happened?" asked Nell.

"Please, Nell," said her father, holding her mother upright, "a fan or a magazine!"

"Yes, yes!"

While his daughter rushed into the parlor, William Ingram shook his head. "Weeds. Damn weeds. Who would've thought?"

Nell returned with a magazine she waved in her mother's face. When Mrs. Ingram opened her eyes, they assisted her to the sofa in the parlor. Nell went to fetch a glass of iced tea.

"Make it a sherry," said her mother, straightening up on the sofa.

Her father nodded in agreement. "There should be some in the study."

Nodding, Nell disappeared down the hallway.

"Was I dreaming?" asked his wife.

"If so, then all your dreams have come true. Your daughter's likely to become the next Belle of Charleston and this afternoon I learned just how much I enjoy weeds."

When Franklin, Senior, passed her house, Sue Ellen hopped on the phone. Conscious that the operator might be listening, she asked, "Do you still have a weed problem?"

"No. I don't think so," said Nell. She was still stunned. What would Rachel Andersen think of this?

Sue Ellen was as high as a kite. There was nothing she couldn't do. Take that, Miss Rachel La-di-dah Belle. "Tomorrow we pick out your dress."

"I don't know . . . I'm not getting my hopes up."

"And the day after that, bridesmaids' dresses."

"No, no, no. This is happening much too fast . . ." Her voice trailed off when the doorbell rang.

"Is it who I think it is?" asked Sue Ellen, knowing that the only phone in the Ingrams' house, like most homes, was in the downstairs hallway.

"Oh, yes. It is! I can't believe he's actually here."

"Why not? Franklin's a gentleman and must make amends for any indiscretions by his father."

But all she heard was a click on the other end of the line.

Sue Ellen put down the phone. Perhaps she'd call the solicitor's office. Now, what good reason would she have to ask to speak to Billy Ray? Something about her father's estate . . .

Yes, yes, that could work.

FIFTEEN

When Tessa Stuart wanted to talk about boys, she slipped into cousin Katie's room after her grandmother had turned out her lights and gone to bed.

Tessa had spent a good number of summers in the upstate, and to tell the truth, Katie, mother of three boys, enjoyed their late-night conversations whether held in Greenville or in Charleston.

"Luke Andersen is terribly cute."

Katie laughed from where she combed her hair. She looked at Tessa in the mirror. "His older brother's cute, so why shouldn't the baby brother be. But I must warn you that there are problems in that marriage."

Tessa straightened up where she sat on the bed.

"These North-South marriages rarely work. I doubt you remember Victoria Roper, who once lived at the Old Maids' Club"—the name given to the boarding house where three old maids raised Katie

Belle before she married Cousin Jimmy. Cousin Jimmy had lodged there, too, in an attempt to catch Katie's eye.

"I remember the Ropers from Sunday dinners."

"That was her second marriage."

"I thought divorce was illegal in South Carolina."

"Depends on the judge. Victoria was originally from Columbus, Ohio. Her first husband was from Charleston, and when they married, Victoria's father disowned her."

Tessa's hand rose to her mouth. "That's just like Rachel."

"These things do happen. You have to remember that Victoria's father lost his father and an uncle in the Civil War. Unfortunately for Victoria, her father was right. The young man turned out to be a ne'er-do-well."

"So I shouldn't date Luke."

"Has he even asked?"

"No, but I see a lot of him at family functions. Uncle James must think highly of him because he let Luke drive one of the trucks north the night before the funeral."

Katie spun around on her stool and shook her hairbrush at Tessa. "Don't remind me. My husband and younger children missing Uncle Jeb's funeral has caused problems in *my* marriage."

Tessa nodded. "Yes, ma'am."

"The point I'm trying to make is, for as long as I've known Rachel Belle, she's never done a day's worth of work, unless it was instructing the help around the house or charity work."

Unfortunately, that could apply to Tessa, who occasionally instructed the help around Ashley Hall and had diligently worked on the library drive organized by Miss McBee, its headmistress.

Katie faced the mirror again. "I'm astonished that Christian's family allowed such a prima donna to live with them for as long as they did. I wanted to ask Rachel about living up north, but she blew up at my article in *Vanity Fair*, so I dropped it."

"I heard she returned from Wisconsin with really red, rough hands and broken nails."

"Well, it is cold up there." Katie chuckled. "At least you've got Luke down here so you won't have to slog through all that ice and snow to catch him."

"Then there's hope?"

"There's always hope." Katie smiled into the mirror again. "You really like this boy, do you?"

Tessa nodded. "I really do. He's a little shy, but I believe I can draw him out. Luke's out of his element in Charleston."

"Have you kissed?"

Tessa shrank back. "Of course not."

"Then you have a chance to keep your senses about you."

"Are you saying . . . are you saying I shouldn't kiss Luke?"

"I'm saying not to forget the old Arabian proverb: When the camel gets his nose in the tent, the rest of his body will soon follow."

"Then don't kiss boys?"

"Don't let boys kiss you like you've seen in the talkies—with passion. You've seen actors kissing in the talkies?"

"Oh, yes. Hartleigh and I used to go all the time, and she really misses it. She's really looking forward to seeing *All Quiet on the Western Front*."

When Al Jolson's *The Jazz Singer* came to Charleston, Hartleigh was instantly smitten, and she continued to see a good number of talkies when she was being courted by James Stuart. Being confined to bed for the last month of her pregnancy made her restless. One day, while waiting in vain for James to appear for their luncheon, she went on a crying jag, babbling on about the loss of her beloved talkies.

Rachel tried to distract her by suggesting that they have some baby clothes sent over for their inspection, but nothing worked.

After a while, Christian became exasperated, not only at Hartleigh but his own wife. "Hartleigh, Stuart and Company is the largest business of its type in South Carolina, and Jeb, Senior, left it in disarray. You should cut your husband some slack."

Rachel turned on him with a viciousness he'd never before experienced, and quite a few choice words Christian had only heard in the warehouse.

Scrambling to his feet and dropping his napkin on the table, Christian said, "I think . . . I think I'd better get back to work."

"Why don't you eat your supper at that damn warehouse," shouted his wife, "maybe sleep on one of those fancy bunk beds."

Christian returned to work, shaking his head. "I told you that you should go home for lunch. You have a problem with your wife."

James looked up from his inventory. The ruins of duck club sandwiches—substituted duck for turkey—lay around him along with their accompanying duck fries, or fries baked in duck fat.

"Should I be at home with her?"

Christian explained what had happened at the luncheon, ending with Hartleigh's complaint that she hadn't seen a talkie in weeks and that she would miss *All Quiet on the Western Front* while it was in town.

James put down his pen, locked up the paper-work, and left the building. This time he didn't take along Alexander or Lewis; instead he took the cop walking the beat outside the warehouse. Leaving the building, James handed a box of the very best scotch to the cop.

"And how do I explain this with me being in uniform?" asked the patrolman.

"Tell them it's confiscated and you're teaching me a lesson about so brazenly displaying illegal liquor."

"I can do that."

Later that day, a projector and its operator arrived at the house where *All Quiet on the Western Front* was shown to a hallway-capacity crowd. Even the widow Stuart came over so she wouldn't be left alone in the big old house next door. Tessa and Luke sat in front and held hands. The projector was set up just inside the front door and a sheet was pinned to the double doors leading to the rear of the house. If anyone dared open those doors, they would hear it from the hallway crowd. Benjamin and Chloe demanded popcorn and sat on either side of Hartleigh in the love seat that had been moved in from the parlor. The demand for popcorn held up the show for at least twenty minutes as a pressure cooker was pressed into service and Molly and Pearl scurried around, searching the pantry for some kernels to pop.

When James came home later that night, Pearl rose out of one of the wicker chairs on the front porch. "Mister James?"

"Oh, hello, Pearl. And how are you tonight?" James was in an excellent mood. He figured he had done pretty well for himself, not to mention that Sue Ellen had seen Aunt Jo off at the train station earlier in the day.

"I want to thank you for that fine talking movie we saw earlier this evening, but I'd like Benjamin to stop watching the house next door. He does have school, you know."

James looked at the boy slumped in one of the wicker rockers. "Would you rather I ask Alexander to watch the house?"

"No, sir, I would not. It's not a good idea for colored men to be lurking in bushes anywhere at anytime."

"Er . . . okay." He glanced at the front door. Coming home was turning into a real minefield. "Benjamin, you heard your mother. No more watching."

"Yes, sir."

"Thank you, Mister James."

"Not at all, Pearl, and I'm happy you enjoyed the talkie."

"Oh, we all had a grand time."

As Benjamin followed his mother into the house, he stuck out his left arm and vigorously pointed at the house next door. Wondering what Benjamin was so agitated about, James walked around the hedge to the house he had grown up in. There, he found his sister with her back to the wall of the wraparound porch, skirt hiked up, and Billy Ray Craven's hands all over her.

Moving quickly but silently, James slipped up

the steps, crossed the porch, and pulled Billy Ray off his sister; the impetuousness of the move all but guaranteeing that Billy Ray would continue backwards, fall over the railing, and land in the poinsettias lining the wraparound porch.

Sue Ellen squealed, pulled down her little black dress, and readjusted her undergarments. She squealed a second time when James grabbed her arm and jerked her around the corner and through the front doors. Before the door closed behind them, they heard Billy Ray cursing as he tried to free himself from the bushes.

"Good God, Sue Ellen! What if Tessa had seen that? They watched a talkie next door tonight."

"What?" asked Sue Ellen, who wasn't focusing all that well. A talkie next door? That didn't make sense. You couldn't watch movies at home.

James pulled his sister up the stairs and across the hallway where he rapped sharply on their mother's bedroom door.

"Who is it?" asked their mother.

Trying to control his anger, James took a breath and let it out. "It's James, Mother. Make yourself decent. I'm coming in."

Sue Ellen couldn't believe she was still on her feet. Her legs felt weak and she couldn't catch her breath. She brushed down her dress again and adjusted her cloche hat.

James opened the door and pulled his sister inside.

Their mother turned on a bedside lamp. She glanced at the clock. "Why are you two still up?"

"Sue Ellen's husband is asking why his wife doesn't join him in New York."

"Does he know that your father recently passed?"

"He knows that—from a week ago. You received a letter of condolence. Have Sue Ellen ready tomorrow morning. I'm sending her to New York."

"And who will care for Mother?" asked Sue Ellen, finally catching her breath.

"Tessa! Alexander will handle transportation out to the new airport. Katie will fly her to New York."

"Is that really safe?" asked their mother.

"Katie flies almost every day, Mother."

"But a girl flying a plane—"

"James," said his sister, "I'm not ready to do this."

"Really, James, must she fly?"

"Well, I can't take off four days or more for a train trip to New York."

"Maybe later then," suggested their mother.

After letting out an exasperated sigh, James said, "The decision has been made, Mother."

"James, I told you I'm not ready to do this."

"All you need is an overnight bag and a change of clothing. The remainder of your clothing will be sent by train."

"James, don't bully your sister."

"Mother, I know this is difficult, but you must let me make the decisions now."

Their mother was quiet for a long moment, then said to Sue Ellen, "It's nothing to worry about. Tessa and I will get along nicely, that is, if James stops by occasionally."

"Don't I breakfast with you every morning?"

"Well, then, maybe it's for the best."

Sue Ellen followed her brother out of the room.

"Good night, Mother," said both of them.

In the hallway, Sue Ellen attacked. "This is so

absolutely mean of you, James."

But James was knocking on a door across the hallway.

In moments, Katie opened the door and pulled tight her robe, eyes full of sleep. "Yes? What is it?"

"Can you fly Sue Ellen to New York in the morning?"

Katie glanced at her cousin across the hall. "I don't know. This is pretty short notice."

"You know that Tin Goose I asked you to check out in case we purchased one for the company?"

Katie's eyes brightened. "Yes?"

"File a flight plan for one of those."

"Gotcha, but nobody flies at night. It's against the law. I'll call early tomorrow. Someone should be there by then."

"Thank you." James reached inside his suit, took out his wallet, and counted out some bills. "Will this cover it?"

Katie checked the count. "Absolutely."

"Is there anything else you need?"

"Tell Jimmy where I've gone. He'll get in even later than you tonight."

"Hartleigh wouldn't believe that if you told her."

Katie laughed and closed the door.

Sue Ellen followed her brother to the head of the stairs. "You really believe you can lord over everyone, don't you?"

From midway down the stairs, her brother looked up. "I know about your trip across the Ashley with Nell Ingram."

His sister blanched, visibly shaken. She gripped the railing to steady herself. "But how?"

"I know everything that goes on in this town—from

people who want to impress me, people who inform on others, or try to misdirect me. It's a holdover from building the bridge."

"Does Hartleigh . . . ?"

"Of course not."

"Thank . . . thank you for that."

"Then you'll be ready in the morning?"

"Yes, sir."

"Sue Ellen, your husband deserves better."

"Better than what?"

"Better than you."

On the front porch Billy Ray waited. "You and I have something to settle, Stuart. We can go somewhere else or hash it out right here."

James took out his wallet again and counted out a series of bills. He handed them to the assistant solicitor, then went down the steps.

"What's this?" asked Billy Ray, following him down the steps.

"Five hundred dollars to just walk away, and if you run for solicitor, there'll be another five hundred on the day you announce."

"Me . . . run for office?"

Opening the wrought-iron gate, James said, "You never liked being number two. I learned that when you played behind me at quarterback in high school."

Billy Ray put away the money. "Really, running for solicitor, I'd have to talk it over with my wife."

"Then do it. Grace has an excellent head on her shoulders." Outside the gate, James extended a hand. "No hard feelings?"

"No hard feelings."

They shook on it.

"James, how about I buy you a drink and you can tell me what you said to Vincenzo Petrocelli so that a full-fledged liquor war didn't break out when your father died."

James glanced at the light still on in his bedroom in the house next door. "Wish I could but I'm expected home sometime tonight."

Hartleigh was still awake when James came in. She put down her book, *Scarlet Sister Mary,* a novel set among the Gullah people of the low country, in which the heroine is torn between being an upright woman or giving in to her baser instincts. Winner of the Pulitzer Prize, the story was turned into a play that ran a mere twenty-four performances.

Without a word, James went to the dresser and swallowed a spoonful of castor oil, his usual routine before giving his wife a kiss on the cheek. But tonight, Hartleigh held his face with her hands when he bent over.

"Ugh! You didn't have to do that, especially tonight."

James smiled. "Turn about is fair play." He poured a glass of water that she sipped to wash away the taste.

"Thank you."

James returned the glass to the nightstand, then took off most of his clothing behind the privacy screen, pulled on a robe, and went to the bathroom.

When he returned, Hartleigh said "I just wish I was more attractive after what you did tonight. Everyone was thrilled with the talkie."

James removed his robe. "I don't know what you mean. I've never seen you look more radiant."

"James," said Hartleigh, as she threw back the covers, "get in this bed right now. We need to do some serious canoodling."

Later, as she lay in his arms, Hartleigh said, "James, there are three women living in that house next door, and Tessa attends Ashley Hall every day."

"You don't think they're safe?"

"I just know we're responsible for them."

"But don't widows live all over Charleston, you know, with a single female servant?"

"Your mother's one of the richest widows in Charleston. That makes her a target of not only gold diggers, but plain old thieves."

James pulled away. "Please don't tell me you're sending me home to live with my mother."

"Don't be silly. I have other plans for you."

"That sounds ominous."

He put his arm around her again and she snuggled in.

"In a day and age when nobody stays at home," explained Hartleigh, "I don't mean they don't call, many do, but everyone goes out for cocktails, dinner, and dancing. I have a lot of catching up to do."

"Is that a threat?"

Hartleigh smiled up at him. "Yes, my dear, it is."

"Does this mean you won't want to immediately get pregnant again?"

"Absolutely not!" And Hartleigh said this so forcefully that she forgot to blush.

"Well, then, what am I to do about Mother?"

"Why don't you have Prescott and Polly Mitchell take a room there? You could convert your father's study into a downstairs bedroom and there's a half-bath across the hall from the study."

"You can't be serious. Prescott's so self-centered nobody can stand him."

"Polly can."

"But I thought we agreed that Polly's nuts."

"James, that's rude."

"You're the one who said it."

"James, please. You can't hold a girl to what she says before she's wed."

"What about love, honor, and obey? That comes before you're pronounced man and wife?"

"I know, I know, but once the minister says 'you may kiss the bride,' husbands have to deal with a new creature. A wife." Hartleigh shifted out of the crook of his arm to lie on her own pillow. "I'll set up a dinner and invite the Mitchells over."

This did not please her husband. "It's totally inappropriate to involve my mother in any social engagements for at least a year. She's a new widow."

"James, this is not your area of expertise." She tried to turn into him, but her tummy stopped her. Instead, she reached out and turned his head toward her. "Just consider the idea. Polly's exceedingly able and Prescott's so crippled that he won't be climbing any stairs and showing up in the wrong bedroom."

James considered this. "You may be right. Mother told me Sue Ellen's leaving for New York in the morning."

Hartleigh pulled away again. "I've heard nothing of this."

"Yeah. I think her decision was kind of sudden."

SIXTEEN

The following day, Sue Ellen complained, "We might be flying, but I feel like I've been railroaded out of Charleston."

From the pilot's seat, Katie raised her voice over the hum of the engine. Her son sat in the copilot seat mesmerized by being in the second seat of a Ford Trimotor. He was studying the instrument panel and referring to a manual lying in his lap, wishing he had a multiengine license like his mom.

"Sorry, but you're a married woman who goes dancing on Sullivan's Island. It's only a matter of time."

"What am I supposed to do . . . stay home every night?"

"This is a great opportunity. In New York City you can become a complete woman."

"I'm already a complete woman. I just don't have a baby yet."

"Cousin, that's not what I meant at all. I'm going to show you a thing or two if I can keep your husband's hands off you long enough."

Before lunch, Christian came in the office with his younger brother. Both were sweating and mopping their faces with handkerchiefs.

"Don't try to change the subject, kiddo. President Hoover is a great man, even putting aside the humanitarian drive to feed occupied Belgium during the war. Let's concentrate on his most recent accomplishment. You're too young to remember, but when the Mississippi broke through its banks and levees in the spring of 1927, the disaster affected millions, and we budding engineering students at the University of Chicago kept up with the disaster by both newspaper and radio. Some professors posted Hoover's progress on their blackboards."

Christian took a seat on the corner of the table where a small fan oscillated. "As Commerce Secretary, Herbert Hoover talked the railroads into transferring displaced people for free, had a fleet of plywood motorboats built to scour the Mississippi for the dead or missing, and helped the Red Cross raise eight million dollars."

"Eight million?" Luke whistled and sat up. A sum that large was incomprehensible.

"Not only that, Hoover had the state governors appoint a dictator to run the local operation that would temporarily resettle the homeless in concentration camps, and wherever he was, Hoover took time to broadcast their progress. We engineering students got the message: the water might be high but hopes were higher, and the South would be all right because the Great Engineer was on the job."

Both men became aware of the look on Lewis's face, and off to one side, one of the collectors' faces lined with worry. Prescott Mitchell sat behind the desk and not in his wheelchair.

"What's going on?" asked Christian.

Luke leaned forward on the bunk bed.

Lewis picked up the phone and dialed a number. "It comes as no surprise to learn that Stuart and Company has a couple of customers who want to do business with Eddie Elliott."

"I imagine he's one of the other bootleggers, right?" asked Christian.

"Probably strong-armed into doing business with him. James went to see Elliott."

"Who went with him?" asked Christian.

"Alexander."

"But they won't allow a Negro into a white man's speak."

"True."

Christian turned to the bagman. "Why didn't you go with him?"

"I'm no enforcer. I just collect."

"Where'd they go?" demanded Christian.

"Elliott's on Market."

Christian went out the door, followed by his brother.

After they left, Lewis said into the phone, "Rogers Sidney. Lewis Belle calling."

"Who's that?" asked Prescott from behind the desk.

Lewis put his hand over the phone. "Imperial Kleagle, or the major recruiter in Charleston County for the Klan." Into the phone, the attorney said, "Yes, Rogers, this is Lewis Belle. I have it on good authority that some colored boy is going to meet his girlfriend—a white girl—at the back door of Elliott's speakeasy when she gets off work."

Lewis listened, then said, "Yes, they're going to try to slip out the back door together." The attorney hung up the phone.

"Pardon me," asked Prescott from behind the desk, "but didn't you just throw Alexander to the wolves."

Lewis was dialing another number. "I'd rather think of it as bailing James out of a tight spot. You can't run Stuart and Company without James Stuart."

Someone on the other end of the line answered.

"Lewis Belle for Antonio Petrocelli."

In a moment, Lewis said into the phone, "You remember what I said about competition, such as Eddie Elliott trying to snake an account or two from Stuart and Company?"

Prescott could hear the bootlegger screaming. "I warned that college boy! Giving away those whorehouses and getting out of the dope business. They'll think he's gone soft."

Lewis held the phone away. When he returned his ear to the receiver, he found himself talking to an empty line. He hung up.

"Why didn't you go with James?" asked Prescott.

"And be caught in the crossfire? Not my style."

"Sounds rather cowardly to me."

"Bootlegging isn't like a tea party," said Lewis. "Petrocelli allied himself with us because we're the largest operation in the state. Eddie Elliott is trying to pick off a couple of accounts. They're small potatoes, but if we don't fight for them, he'll go for larger ones."

Lewis got up and stretched. He looked around.

"Where's your chair?" Lewis had found the wheelchair to be much more comfortable than any other chair in the room. Why not? Cripples spent their lives in them.

"It squeaks. Alexander said he'd oil it."

Lewis stared at where the chair usually stood. "You don't think . . ."

Three cars full of Petrocelli's men raced down Meeting Street. In the lead car, Petrocelli cursed James Stuart as "that damn college boy."

"Then why are we helping him, boss?"

"Balance of power. Status quo. Honestly, Bruno, don't you ever listen or are you just looking for your next fight?"

"I listen, boss." And to make his point, Bruno took out his pistol and checked the load.

Petrocelli shook his head. "For over ten years, I've kept the peace. Well, Jeb Stuart and I've kept the peace, and the only time I ever worried was when Jeb started consuming his own product."

The car took a hard left on Market Street, and Petrocelli held out a hand to brace himself. "If anything, the Stuarts owe me a percentage for handling this."

Bruno nodded. "We'll make 'em pay, boss. You can count on me to back your play."

Petrocelli rolled his eyes before the three cars screeched to a stop in front of Elliott's speakeasy. Before getting out, he said, "Just keep your gat in its holster."

"Er . . . yes, boss."

SEVENTEEN

Alexander stopped the Buick down the street from the speakeasy, got out, and opened the trunk. He pulled out the wheelchair, opened it—James sat down—and rolled him over to the door. After James knocked, a peephole opened over his head.

From inside, a voice said, "No colored."

James rose up on the chair's arms. "James Stuart to see Eddie Elliott." He sat back down. While the peephole closed and the door unlocked, James muttered, "This is so inconvenient."

"Do say," said Alexander. "And Mister Prescott will spend the rest of his life in one of these things."

The door of the speakeasy opened, and a large man with no neck stepped back so Alexander could roll the chair in.

"My mistake, Captain Stuart. Please come in."

Alexander rolled the chair down a long hall to a left turn where another bodyguard waited. The room behind the man was filled with tables and chairs, along with laughing and dancing patrons. Smoke filled the air and waitresses walked the floor with trays of drinks. Scantily clad girls offered cigarettes from roped trays hanging around their necks. At the rear of the room was a long bar lined with customers, and at the front center, a small jazz band played "Happy Days Are Here Again." Chandeliers lit the room, heavy drapes softened the light, and the noise level made it almost impossible to hear.

James shook his head. "Hard to believe a hillbilly built all this."

When the bodyguard bent down, James repeated his demand to see Elliott. The bodyguard said he would have to check with the boss, and Alexander and James watched him climb stairs leading to a second-story door that opened behind a curtain.

Still admiring the joint, James shook his head. "And this guy wants to be a bootlegger."

A blonde came over and asked if she could seat them.

James shook his head.

The blonde evaluated Alexander. "Well, aren't you the big fellow."

"I'm married."

The blonde jerked a thumb over her shoulder. "Most of these fellers are, too, but that never seems to slow them down."

After she sauntered off, bottom twitching, James said, "You won't get very far with that sort of pick-up line."

Alexander only grunted.

A moment later, the bodyguard descended the stairs and walked over to them. Raising his voice, he said, "Mister Elliott will see you upstairs."

Staring up the stairs, James said, "How inconsiderate of him."

"What?" asked the bodyguard, bending down.

But Alexander had pushed away, negotiating the wheelchair between chairs and tables, and over to the stairs. People made way and watched them go.

Alexander looked up the stairs and James looked up at him. James smiled and Alexander let out a long sigh before scooping him up.

Halfway up the stairs, James said, "You know, I could get used to this."

"Don't" was Alexander's one-word reply.

The door to the office was opened by another large, no-neck man in a business suit. Alexander carried James into a small but elaborately decorated office with lots of curtains and dim lights. Behind the desk sat a freckled-face, middle-aged man in a three-piece suit. On a sofa sat a blonde in a red dress. She smoked a cigarette in a holder and eyed the newcomers.

"Captain Stuart, and what do I owe . . ." was all Elliott got out before James slipped out of Alexander's arms and hauled out two Webley Mk VI revolvers from under his jacket. The Webley Mk VI had proved to be a hardy and reliable weapon in the muddy trenches of the Great War. Now James pointed one at Elliott and one at his bodyguard.

Alexander backed away, and when the bodyguard foolishly pulled his weapon, James shot him in the leg. The large man went down, dropping his pistol and grabbing his leg. James glanced at the girl and kicked away the pistol. Alexander was locking the door and Elliott was reaching inside a drawer when James stepped over and stuck a pistol in his face.

"Hands behind your head!"

Elliott pulled his hand out of the drawer and placed his hands behind his head. "You're not getting away with this."

James pointed at the blonde with his other pistol. "Undress!"

The blonde didn't seem to understand.

James stepped in her direction, the pistol leading the way. "*Undress!*"

The girl nodded and put down her cigarette. She scrambled off the sofa and started pulling off her clothing. When she got down to her underwear, she looked frantically at Elliott.

"Bare skin, honey," confirmed James. "Unwrap yourself."

Alexander had knelt beside the bodyguard, pulled off the man's belt, and secured it around his thigh. "Mister James, this man's going to bleed to death if we don't get him to a hospital."

Instead, James kept an eye on Elliott but spoke to the girl. "Get over in the corner, lady, near the door!"

The blonde picked up her clothes and headed for the door.

"Leave the clothing."

"But . . . but . . ."

James's eyes remained on Elliott as he instructed the girl. "Drop the clothing, strip off your underwear, and stand in the corner until you receive further instructions."

The blonde paused before stripping off the cloth wrapped around her chest as fashion dictated, then pulled off her underwear and garter belt. No one was looking. All eyes were on the two Webleys.

"You are stupid," said James, moving around Elliott's desk to confront the man.

"I'm the stupid one? You'll never get out of here alive."

"You had a nice little business going here, but you just had to become a bootlegger. Stay in the nightclub business, Eddie. Not only are you good at it, but you'll live to tell the tale."

"You can't come in here and tell me what to do."

"Oh, really?" James stepped closer and forced Elliott back. "I own the cops in this town, but most importantly, I'm the one who conned your people into allowing me to get this close. You don't think I can't do it again?"

"Next time I'll be ready for you."

"Oh, really," said James, swinging one of the pistols around and pointing it at the wounded bodyguard. "You really think your security people are up to the task?"

"Mister James," said Alexander, "this man needs to go to the hospital."

The bodyguard moaned as blood puddled on the floor.

James moved a pistol to one side of Elliott's head. "Next time I'm forced to deal with you, I'm going to discharge a pistol right beside your head and you'll never hear out of that ear again."

"I won't take this—"

James tapped Elliott on the side of the head. "Listen up!"

Elliott winced and backed away.

"Either agree or we stand here and watch your man bleed to death."

From the floor came: "Boss, please . . ."

Without taking his eyes off the bootlegger, James pocketed one of the Webleys and rifled through the desk drawers with his free hand. He came up with a pistol and a couple of journals. The pistol he jammed into his belt, the journals he put under his arm.

"You can't take those. My whole business is in there."

"You want them, come and get them tomorrow at the Stuart and Company warehouse."

"I'm not that stupid."

"Then bring along the chief of police."

"I don't think the chief's in my pocket like he is yours."

James smiled. "Now you get the picture. Do you agree to my terms?"

"Under threat of being shot, what other choice do I have?"

"I'm not shooting you. I'll leave that for a friend of your bodyguard when they learn you allowed him to bleed to death."

"Boss," groaned the bodyguard, "please . . ."

Elliott looked at the wounded man, then bit his lip. "Agreed."

"No more bootlegging."

It was a moment before Elliott said, "Agreed."

"Alexander, pick up that guy and wait at the door."

"You'll never get out of this building alive."

"Oh, I don't think anyone will notice." James motioned with a revolver at the blonde who had covered her chest and groin with her hands and huddled near the door. "Out the door, honey."

She glanced at the door. "Go down there naked?"

"Do it!"

The girl did, unlocking the door and opening it. With Alexander helping the wounded bodyguard down the stairs, the naked woman timidly started down the steps, but when the wolf whistles started, she finished the stairs in a rush.

Elliott followed Alexander because of the pistol stuck in his back. He held his hands up but no one seemed to notice. First, men craned their heads, then, when the naked woman ran out the door and down the long hallway toward the front, all of them followed. Wives and girlfriends were left in the lurch.

Alexander pushed the wounded bodyguard in the wheelchair, and James shoved Elliott ahead of him by holding onto the man's belt. Behind them came a mob of men trying to push their way past and reach the girl. At the door, the bodyguard stood stock still as everyone rushed forward. He opened the door for the woman, who, once outside, ran into the arms of Bruno.

When James exited the speakeasy, Petrocelli asked, "What the hell's going on in there?"

"Eddie and his bodyguard need a ride to Roper. Can you take them?"

Petrocelli looked around at the assembling crowd, not only those from inside the speakeasy but those on the street who stopped and stared.

"Anything to get away from this."

Men continued to stream out of the speak as Bruno covered the girl with his jacket. Passersby stopped and stared.

"Phyllis?" asked Bruno, holding the girl out from him. "Is that you?"

Once the blonde had the jacket around her, she threw herself into Bruno's arms again. "Oh, take me

CHARLESTON'S HOUSE OF STUART

away from here, cousin. Please, and I promise I'll never, ever come back to this place."

Bruno looked at Petrocelli, Petrocelli nodded, and Bruno escorted Phyllis over to one of the three cars.

Before leaving, Bruno said to James, "You watch yourself, college boy."

"Hey," said James, smiling, "I'm like the rest of the guys. I'm watching your cousin."

Bruno almost released the girl to take a poke at James, but stopped when James opened his jacket to reveal the two Webleys and Elliott's pistol.

Petrocelli said, "Get in the car, Bruno."

The girl was bawling, practically hysterical, as men groped her. Bruno hustled her into the car, brushing away hands as he did.

The wounded bodyguard had been lifted into the rear of the second car and sat there holding his leg and moaning. Before getting inside, Eddie Elliott straightened up and announced that he didn't need any ride to the hospital.

Petrocelli punched the speakeasy owner in the face. "Oh, yes you do." And he pushed Elliott into the backseat of the second car.

Once Petrocelli was seated inside the car, he rolled down his window. "Stuart, did you know there's a squad of cops at the back door of this joint?"

"No," said James, glancing in that direction, "but that seems about right." He thumped the top of the sedan and the car pulled away while onlookers drifted into the street, into the wake of three cars.

As Alexander stowed the wheelchair in the trunk, Christian and Luke came running down the street.

Before he completely caught his breath, Christian asked, "What's . . . what's . . . going on . . . here?"

"Nothing much," said James, strapping in the Webleys and closing his jacket. He handed Elliott's pistol to the Yankee. "Just another sales call."

* * *

Within months of the stock market crash, Walter Waters had lost his job at the cannery, and in a matter of weeks, he had become a "fruit tramp," or itinerant worker who goes from one harvest to the next. Saddled with debts he could never pay off, Walter hung around the VFW where he occasionally found leads for his next job. To make sure he nailed down one of those jobs, Walter would immediately began hiking toward his next opportunity, even in the middle of the night. Some leads turned out to be bogus, so Walter would return to the VFW for another beer and another tip.

During the Great War, Walter had served in France, so sooner than later the conversation would turn to the possibility that the government might pay veterans the long-promised enlistment bonus ten years early.

Still, in 1930, this was only talk, and two of the people talking the loudest were Governor Huey Long of Louisiana, who promised to tax the rich and to share the wealth, and a Catholic priest in Detroit, Father Coughlin, who railed against communism, the wealthy, and Prohibition. More and more radio listeners were turning to these two men because both promised to use the power of the government to humble the rich and redistribute the wealth. But still, at this point, it was only talk.

EIGHTEEN

Between Georgiana's hovering and the friends who wanted to welcome Rachel back to Charleston, Hartleigh and Rachel rarely had time to sit down and catch up. But they did pass each other making their many trips to the bathroom, and at a late lunch they finally got to chat, and the subject of the conversation went well beyond Hartleigh asking Rachel what it was like to live up north. There were more recent fish to fry.

"What do you make of your brother and Nell Ingram?"

"I believe she caught him fair and square. I have to respect that in any woman."

"And it doesn't bother you that Nell will move into your home at a time when you're not welcome there?"

"I think my brother was lucky to have someone feign an interest in him."

"Then you don't believe any of this business about the weeds."

"And neither does my mother, but I've cautioned her that whenever she feels the desire to speak out, she should remember that our side of the Belle family will remain in our house on South Battery for at least another generation, maybe two. I'm just envious that this whole scheme was engineered by Sue Ellen and not me. What I suspect is Sue Ellen didn't care a fig about Nell or Franklin. It was the challenge that attracted her."

"Yes," said Hartleigh, after sipping from her iced tea, "I'm often surprised whenever my sister-in-law displays any degree of concern for anyone other than herself."

"With her in New York now, I doubt we'll know the truth of the matter and no one wants to upset the apple cart by quizzing Nell." Rachel sipped her tea and looked at Hartleigh over her glass. "Katie believes your husband had something to do with it."

"I know James is concerned about his sister's reputation."

"Katie's point was that girls don't usually leave town so abruptly unless . . ."

Hartleigh checked the doors, then in a low voice finished, "In the family way."

Rachel put down her glass. "My grandmother used to say that there's usually one girl in every generation who moves in with her aunt in Atlanta or her cousins in Spartanburg, then returns home as virginal as the day she left." Rachel flashed a grim smile. "She cautioned me not to be that girl."

"As did my mother."

After a bite of a crescent roll, Rachel said, "I guess it doesn't matter whether we were good girls or not, now that we're married."

"Rachel, if you think I'm going to share the details of my wedding night, you've got another think coming."

"Yes, yes, I'm sure we were all good girls until our wedding night."

"And that night I hope we were all good wives."

Rachel laughed, then leaned back making her abdomen more prominent. "We must've been. Look at our condition!"

Both laughed long and loud enough to draw the attention of Pearl, who stuck her head in the dining room.

"What trouble you girls getting into in here?"

Both young women pushed back from the table and held out their arms.

"What more trouble could we be in?" asked Hartleigh.

Once Pearl returned to the kitchen, Rachel and Hartleigh went through a period of not being able to stop giggling.

Finally, Hartleigh caught her breath, "I believe . . . we've been pregnant too long."

"Yes, yes, if this keeps up . . . my water may break."

"Oh, no," laughed Hartleigh, "water, water everywhere . . ."

They were swept up in another gale of laughter, and it was a moment before they calmed down and could return to their meal.

"Christian and I really appreciate you taking us in."

"Think nothing of it."

"No, no, no, Hartleigh! We will forever be in your debt."

"Rachel, that's what friends are for." Her tone

changed. "But I have been curious as to what Christian thinks of your father's decision to disinherit you."

"He thought it was a joke."

"He didn't!"

"And I didn't enlighten him."

"Seriously?" Hartleigh's fork stopped in midair.

"My brother inherits everything, so what's the point?"

"You haven't even discussed it with him?"

"I don't think Christian dares raise the subject," said Rachel, dabbing at her mouth with her napkin. "The Andersen family was split over the milk and cheese issue."

"Cheese and butter both come from milk, so why doesn't everyone just produce more milk?"

"My sentiments exactly," said Rachel, laying her napkin across her lap, "but we'd both be wrong. The big producers control the price, especially when it comes to condensed milk sold in grocery stores.

"It's like the Tariff of Abomination in 1828 that was enacted to protect American manufacturing. It wasn't until South Carolina threatened to leave the Union that Congress reduced the tariff, not once but twice. Christian's family has no idea that the War Between the States originated with the tariff. Yankees believe the war was fought over slavery, but it was the high tariffs slapped on foreign goods that made it nearly impossible for the South to purchase manufactured goods from England."

She smiled. "But that's all behind us now. We're back in Charleston where we belong, and Christian's been out looking at houses. He's doing what's called 'leg work.' "

" 'Leg work?' My goodness but that has a rough sound to it."

"I know," said Rachel with a sly smile, "but our generation is supposed to be much more brazen than the previous ones."

"Please," said Hartleigh, mockingly serious, "not us ladies living south of Broad."

"Certainly not. We ladies pick and choose how vulgar we wish to be. Anyway, when they don't come home for the luncheon, Christian and Luke are out evaluating a house and bringing home sketches."

"A side benefit of marrying an engineer."

"So, once the babies arrive, we'll be out of your hair. Who knows? Georgiana may move in with us. When Christian and I had dinner there, we made it clear that she was always welcome. It's certainly good to have your mother around when you deliver."

Rachel realized what she had said. "Oh, I'm sorry. That was rather insensitive of me."

Hartleigh's mother was on a grand tour of Europe, and with her daughter married to James Stuart, Elizabeth Randolph had little interest in returning to Charleston. Five years earlier, a ferry boat accident had devastated the Randolph family; in it Hartleigh's father had drowned, as had her younger brother and twin sister, Mary Anne. This had happened only weeks before Mary Anne was to announce her engagement to James Stuart. Four years later, when James returned to Charleston to build the bridge and turned his attention to Hartleigh, Elizabeth Randolph had refused to sanction their engagement or their marriage.

To change the subject, Rachel asked, as she cut into her meat, "Why serve so much hamburger?"

"To economize—oh, I'm sorry, would you prefer another choice of meat?"

"Oh, no, when in Rome . . ."

"Then we shall have something entirely different tomorrow."

"Don't go out of your way on my account. I'm just pleased to have a roof over our heads."

"Oh, my, I never thought . . ." Hartleigh put down her fork. "When you returned to Charleston, you certainly expected more of our traditional Charleston fare." Today the kitchen had served hamburger steak with onions and brown gravy, hot white rice, and fried okra. Carrot cake would be for dessert.

"Well," said Rachel, smiling, "I could stand shrimp and grits more than once a week."

"Done!"

Another gale of laughter followed, and because of that, they failed to hear Rachel's mother and Nell Ingram enter the house. Nell had been too skittish to simply drop by, and for this reason she had enlisted the support of Georgiana. What rattled Nell was the fact that Sue Ellen had tricked Rachel's brother into proposing marriage, and the next day Sue Ellen had left town like some pregnant teenager.

Hearing the laughter in the dining room, Georgiana drifted in that direction, only to be horrified to hear what her daughter said next. Both women became as motionless and as quiet as statues.

From the dining room, they heard Rachel say, "There's another favor I wish to ask."

Hartleigh dabbed at her mouth with her napkin. "Anything."

"Christian and I wish to accompany you and James to Saint Michael's on Sunday."

"Really? But you're a Huguenot."

"And Christian is a Lutheran. But we've decided to raise the children as Episcopalians."

"Rachel, this is a big decision. Are you sure?"

"Believe me, like the milk war in the Andersen household, this issue has been talked to death."

Georgiana could not believe what she was hearing. She put a hand on the wall to steady herself. Nell gripped Georgiana's arm.

In the dining room, Hartleigh said, "You know I must discuss this with James."

"As I would expect you to do."

Georgiana eased into one of the hallway chairs, her breath coming fast and furious. Afraid that the older woman might hyperventilate, Nell held open her purse and encouraged Georgiana to breathe into it.

"You really think your father would object to sharing the Belle pew with you and your husband."

Rachel put down her fork. "I know the reasonable thing would be for us to take a rear pew, but how would we explain that to the twins? Your grandparents sit up front, but we sit in the rear of the church." She picked up her fork again. "This is just one of those silly decisions my father made without considering the consequences."

Molly came through the swinging door and went around the table, refilling their glasses. "Heard there was a party in here."

"Just a couple of laughing jackasses," said Rachel.

Hartleigh held up her hands. "Don't get me started."

"Anything I can get for you ladies?"

Rachel said that everything was fine and her compliments to the chef. In the hallway, Georgiana was helped to her feet by her future daughter-in-law. She and Nell staggered out of the house.

Secrets and deceit, thought Nell as they went out the door. Nothing special there. Just your typical south of Broad family.

In the dining room, Hartleigh asked, "Do you think we could have shrimp and grits tomorrow?"

Molly laughed. "Of course. It's high time those babies of yours were swimming in grits."

NINETEEN

The most tragic figure in the Pantheon of the House of Stuart was, hands down, Tessa Stuart. Raised jointly by members of the Stuart family, Tessa had no guiding star but Ashley Hall. For this reason, she chose to become the perfect Charleston lady. But Tessa was still a Stuart and the sea brought out her reckless nature. Fortunately, Tessa was usually at sea when she was at her most unladylike, or spending the summer in Greenville with Katie Stuart, who had taught Tessa how to ride a horse like a man. That's not all Tessa learned while in Greenville.

When Tessa was in Charleston, her actions were above reproach, but in Greenville she ran with a gang of girls who never expected to be presented at Greenville Cotillion. In Greenville, Tessa learned to smoke, drink, and shoplift. But the week before her return to Charleston, Tessa would cover her hands with lotion, don a pair of gloves, and hide from the sun. And once back in Charleston, she pridefully had little to do with anyone connected to the upstate.

But like Rachel Belle, Tessa had been smitten by a tall, blond young man who had been thrust into the bosom of her family. And when Tessa wished to spend more time with Luke Andersen, she asked Nell Ingram and Franklin Belle to chaperone them up the river to Cooper Hill. There, the Belle family had horses and plenty of riding trails, and were close enough to the woods that Franklin could sketch for hours and Nell could size up the estate her children would inherit. There were also plenty of woods where a young couple on horseback could get lost for hours.

So Franklin borrowed James's yacht, and the four of them took a picnic lunch and sailed up the Cooper. Onboard, Tessa sprang into action as Nell was a lady and Luke had never been on any craft larger than a rowboat.

Passing Nell while moving about, the older girl cautioned, "Really, Tessa, I'm not sure a lady should be functioning like a common deckhand."

"Don't worry," said Tessa, holding up her hands to reveal her soiled white gloves, "I brought along another pair."

The girl's reply put Nell off her stride, and it wasn't until Tessa made a second pass that Nell revised her tactics.

"What I mean is that your friend, Luke, isn't being attended to properly, and you are responsible for his comfort."

Holding down her riding dress, which still had a tendency to billow, Tessa looked at Luke. The boy had not moved from where he sat below the mainsail.

"I see what you mean." And Tessa joined Luke as the young man nervously watched the river fly by.

"First time on a boat?" she asked, taking a seat with an assist from Luke.

"Yeah. I guess it shows."

"My ancestors were pirates. I grew up on these waters." Tessa scanned the harbor behind them. "I'm so glad you could get the afternoon off. This will be fun."

"I wanted to ask, you live at Ashley Hall—what's that?"

"It's the only girls' college-preparatory school in the state. All the Belle girls have attended, as have many of the Stuarts."

"Is it that special?"

"I'd say so. From the day you move in, the teachers and the upperclassmen drill you in the goal of Ashley Hall graduates."

"And that is?"

"To produce well-educated women who are independent, ethically responsible, and prepared to face the challenges of society with confidence."

Luke smiled. "You closed your eyes when you recited that."

"I can quote the Ashley Hall mission in my sleep. Ask your sister-in-law. Or even Hartleigh. It's not something you're likely to forget."

Luke glanced toward the stern. "When we sailed under the bridge, I got to thinking that Christian went off to the university, so maybe I should go to Chicago and get an education. Nobody makes money farming. It's been that way for years, and we have an uncle who's a circuit court judge. He does pretty well for himself."

"You could do that in Charleston: attend the Citadel." Tessa raised her voice. "Uncle Franklin, didn't you graduate from the Citadel before you worked on the new bridge?"

"That I did," said Franklin from the helm. To Luke, it seemed that Tessa Stuart had a good number of uncles, not all related by blood.

"See what I mean. You could attend the Citadel during the week, and on the weekends, I could teach you how to sail." More smiles.

"Those boys in uniform I see around town—"

"Cadets. The bald heads belong to the knobs, or first-year men." Then, rather dreamily, she added, "I just love a man in uniform."

Luke had grown up reading about "Black Jack" Pershing, the most famous general of the age, but when you discussed war in Charleston, it wasn't the Great War or the Spanish-American War. It was the Civil War, although Charlestonians had another name for it: The War Between the States.

Christian had warned Luke never to allow himself to be drawn into a discussion about that war, and in the couple of scrapes he'd gotten into, Luke couldn't tell if he was fighting over something he'd said or the fact that he was from up north.

Charlestonians took offense at the least little thing. It wasn't that men didn't fight in Wisconsin— they did, but only as a last resort. This was about the same time Luke noticed that Christian never backed down, not like he would in Wisconsin.

When Luke asked Christian about this, his brother had simply said, "Win or lose, I'll still be able to hold up my head."

The question was: Did Luke Andersen want to live down south? He'd already heard the locals complain about Yankee boys coming south to steal their women. And his brother had done just that. Maybe it wouldn't be such a good idea to spend too much time with Tessa Stuart, though she was awfully smart for a Southern girl and plenty attractive.

"You know," said Tessa, with a wan smile, "Charlestonians have been swimming in these waters for generations. Many times I have, too."

"We have rivers and lakes all over Wisconsin. My friends and I would go . . ." Luke flushed and looked away.

Tessa did not, no, not a sailor's daughter. "Are you saying you didn't always wear a bathing suit?"

Luke's face burned. "I don't think anyone in Wisconsin owns a bathing suit, except maybe those living near Lake Michigan."

Tessa laughed. "I would hope so." She took his hand and forced him to look her in the eye. "Luke, I was a child before I was a lady." She gestured at where Nell had sat before going below. Charleston ladies did not sunburn. "I, too, swim without a bathing suit. I mean, think about it." She tossed her auburn curls. "My hair looks about the same whether I've been swimming or not."

"Really?" But Luke wasn't thinking about the girl's curls.

She released his hand. "Don't worry, nobody's around when I do it."

"I would hope not."

Tessa slapped his knee. "Why? Do you think boys would find me ugly?"

"Oh, no, no, no." And the idea of spending too much time with Tessa Stuart washed away like a sand castle under an assault from a rising tide.

"Someday, you must do it in the ocean: running

along the beach, in and out of the surf, and the moonlight reflected off the water. It's liberating. I used to, but most of my girlfriends have outgrown all that."

Luke was fascinated. He'd never discussed anything like this with a girl. Sure, he'd kissed a few, but he'd never really talked about anything more than to agree that parents were old fogies and the future held much more promise than the older generation believed.

"Where do you swim?" he asked, anxious that this conversation should not end.

Tessa looked downriver. "Not the harbor. It's too filthy. Sullivan's Island's best, though I've always wondered about the Isle of Palms. But I couldn't go there by myself."

"I'll take you." *Now, where had that come from?*

Tessa leaned away from him. "You'd take me?" She glanced at Franklin, who didn't appear to remember that they were still aboard. "We'd do it on the Isle of Palms?"

"I just need a car."

"I can furnish the car. It's just that I've never been to the Isle of Palms in the dark."

"Don't worry," said Luke, emboldened. "I'll bring along a flashlight."

* * *

Sue Ellen's husband, Edward Hall, and Nicholas Eaton shared a suite at the Algonguin Hotel, and since the two men were at work, Katie, without even freshening up, tipped the bellboy a fiver and hustled the bellboy and Sue Ellen back into the hall.

"Thank you, ma'am!"

"Just keep an eye on my son, Roy. He likes to ramble."

With two fingers, the young man saluted her. "You can count on me, Mrs. Stuart."

Katie took Sue Ellen's arm and tugged her toward the elevator. "Come on! They're right downstairs."

"Who? My husband?"

Jebbie stood at the open door of his and his mother's room next door.

"Don't leave the room," said his mother as they passed him. "We'll be back in an hour or so."

"Where you going?" asked the boy.

"The Rose Room."

"Doesn't sound like any place I'd want to go."

Katie continued walking down the hall backwards. "That's why I packed that new detective novel by Dashiell Hammett. Check the bottom of your suitcase." Stopping at the elevator, she added, "Something about a falcon."

"Oh, man, not another book about birds. I really don't care about nature. Why not a book about planes?"

"Give it a try, but stay in your room. Listen to the radio. Better yet, place a long distance call to the Old Maids' Club and tell them that we arrived safe and sound."

Roy asked Jeb if he wanted a soda.

"You mean a Coke?"

"We have that, too." The bellboy stepped inside. "Let's call room service. They could send up a sandwich." The last thing Katie and Sue Ellen heard before the door closed was Roy saying: "*The Maltese Falcon* is definitely not a bird book."

The elevator dinged, the doors opened, and the two women stepped aboard. Its operator sat on a tall stool.

"The Rose Room," said Katie.

The operator punched a button and then pulled the doors closed.

"Is this another fix-up by my brother?"

"No, no. It's the Roundtable."

"What in the world are you talking about? Like in King Arthur?"

"No, silly, like Dorothy Parker and Alexander Woollcott."

"Dorothy Parker, the communist?"

From his seat on the stool, the operator smiled.

"Oh, Sue Ellen, don't be so provincial. You're in New York now. Dorothy's a critic, poet, and short story writer. Matter of fact, they're all writers, editors, or critics."

"Listen, Katie, James is the big reader in the family, not me. I don't have time to read."

"But you've heard of Alexander Woollcott."

"He talks about books on the radio, and that's my point: You can learn anything by listening to the radio."

Again the elevator operator grinned.

"Just don't let Dorothy Parker hear you say that. She'll open you up from gut to gullet."

At that, the operator laughed out loud.

Just as Katie had said, they found the members of the Algonquin Round Table in the Rose Room.

Woollcott saw them coming. "Katie Stuart, as I live and breathe, what a great honor to have you in our fair city again."

Under her breath, Katie said, "They accept me because I've written for *Vanity Fair*."

Parker smiled. "Lady Lindy has returned!"

"And I can hold up my end of a conversation." Katie introduced Sue Ellen to everyone. "A Stuart by blood, not marriage as I am."

"Welcome, fellow Stuart," said Woollcott. "Do have a seat."

Sue Ellen was appalled that none of the men stood, though Harold Ross, introduced as the editor of *The New Yorker*, half rose from his chair. Sitting beside him was his wife, Jane Grant, not the only woman at the table who had kept her maiden name. Strange.

Once they had seated themselves, Katie said, "It would appear your table has lost a few of its members."

"And," said Harold Ross, "I'm about to lose Dottie to Hollywood."

"It's the end of *The New Yorker*," said Woollcott, chuckling. "Harold will print anything written by our fair Dorothy,"

"Yes," said a man introduced as playwright George F. Kaufman, "but only if it's about suicide, melancholia, or divorce."

Everyone laughed, including Parker.

"Don't listen to these people," said Parker. "They're nothing but a bunch of loudmouths and second-tier writers. What's your claim to fame, Sue Ellen Hall?"

Heywood Broun, a sportswriter, waved a warning finger from the other side of the table. "Thin ice, thin ice."

His wife, Ruth Hale, merely shook her head.

"I'm married to one of the engineers building the

Empire State Building. I came up for a visit."

The waiter placed a glass of water and a luncheon menu in front of the newcomers. Silverware and linen napkins were also laid out.

"So you're married," said Parker. "That's your story?"

Woollcott rolled his eyes, knowing what was coming.

"Strike one," called out Heywood Broun.

"Heywood!" said his wife, "she's a newcomer."

Sue Ellen was taken aback. How dare this communist treat her with such distain? After all, she was an eleventh generation Charlestonian.

"I'm a descendant of James Stuart, who killed Blackbeard the pirate."

Again Parker laughed, and those around the table leaned forward, watching Dorothy close in for the kill.

"Still defining yourself by the men in your life, are you?"

"Strike two," announced Broun with a broad grin. "One more strike and you are out of here."

Beside him, his wife wearily shook her head.

Kaufman turned to Katie. "You know the rules, my dear. Be quick, be smart, but most of all don't be boring."

Sue Ellen remembered what her mother had said about true friends, not that any of these people would qualify, but her mother had said that you don't have a true friend unless you share secrets.

"Although I'm a descendant of a founding family, I've been kicked out of Charleston for being too wild."

Everyone laughed, many cheered, and the patrons outside the Rose Room stopped and peeked inside.

Kaufman clapped Sue Ellen on the back. "Bravo, Mrs. Hall, bravo!"

"Now you've elevated yourself to an interesting person," said Parker, "and you'll suffer the slings and arrows that accompany that."

"Gladly," said Katie for a puzzled Sue Ellen.

Ruth Hale had been applauding. "I knew you had it in you, Sue Ellen."

Heywood Broun toasted her. "Another Zelda joins the table! Welcome."

Still, by the end of the lunch both Sue Ellen and Katie were exhausted.

"Lord," said Katie, holding the elevator railing as they rode to their floor, "the brainpower—the wit—at that table. I could barely keep up."

"And me," said Sue Ellen, "I'm going to have to spend a lot more time at the library."

Katie laughed. "But at long last, you're home."

TWENTY

When his wife didn't show up to listen to their usual evening radio programs, Franklin Belle went looking for her and found Georgiana smoking on the back porch.

"Oh, there you are."

Georgiana said nothing.

"You're smoking again?" he asked. "I thought you quit."

She dropped the cigarette to the deck of the screened-in back porch and stepped on it. "I did."

Without another word, she left him wondering what was wrong. Georgiana never missed an episode of *Amos 'n' Andy*.

A pebble hit Tessa's window. Tessa, who had borrowed Hartleigh's copy of *Scarlet Sister Mary*, was engrossed in the story, so it took a second pebble to snap her back into the real world.

Tessa turned out the light, scrambled out of bed,

and hurried to the window. When she looked out, a flashlight beam struck her in the face.

"Ready?" came the hoarse whisper.

"Be right down."

Tessa closed the window, slipped into a pair of Mary Janes, and headed for her door, taking down a wrap. She glanced at her dresser.

Should she take along her bathing suit?

No. Not tonight. Tonight, she was swimming free, and naked as an egg. It was exciting. She'd never done it with a boy before.

Tessa turned the handle and eased open the door. Hearing no one in the central bath and seeing her grandmother's door shut, she crossed the hall and went down the stairs, legs spread wide. Stairs didn't creak if you put your feet at opposite sides.

At the bottom of the stairs, she stopped and listened. The door to Prescott and Polly's room, which had formerly been her grandfather's study, stood open. It always stood open as a condition of the free room and board for the Mitchells. When she heard Prescott snoring, Tessa was out the door and on the front porch where Luke held out his hand to go down the steps.

"Not so fast." Tessa went over to one of the wicker chairs and took a basket from behind it. She handed the basket to Luke. "Who ever heard of going swimming without a picnic lunch."

"Swell."

She took his hand and they went down the steps and out to the Cadillac parked on the street. Luke seated her in the passenger side front seat and placed the picnic basket on the backseat on top of a blanket she'd left there earlier in the day.

As he got into the car, Tessa said, "I have towels in the basket."

Luke chuckled. "You think of everything."

She gripped his hand as she handed him the key. "Luke, you must take care of me tonight. There's no trolley service, no grand hotel, and no rooms for changing. It's very primitive on the Isle of Palms."

Nervous as a cat until this very moment, Luke leaned over and gave her a hug. "You don't have anything to worry about." Luke considered kissing her, but that might really give the girl something to worry about. Anyway, plenty of time for that later.

He fired up the engine, and they drove in silence through the city and over the new bridge. Minutes later, they had crossed the Cooper, then onto Sullivan's Island where they crossed another bridge to the Isle of Palms. The only lights were those in the distance and the very few on Sullivan's Island.

Tessa stared into a darkness that ate up their headlights. It was really dark, and creepy. She slipped across the seat and sat as close to Luke as possible, well, as close as she could and not be in the way of his operating the gearshift. Beneath their tires, the shells crunched as they rolled along.

"People thought the new bridge would develop the Isle of Palms, but the Panic knocked the stuffing out of investors, though I do believe Uncle James has invested over here."

"Christian owns a lot. The bank gave him a real good deal, and . . . oh, I believe we turn right . . . here."

"Oh," said Tessa, finding comfort in his words. "You've been out here before?"

"When we were looking for houses for Rachel."

"Really? They would live in this godforsaken

place? I can understand Sullivan's Island, but here?"

"No," laughed Luke as he peered through the windshield. There was a clump of palmetto trees just ahead, then a line of surf. "During lunch, we look for houses for Rachel. One day we drove out here to check a lot on the water. We were making a delivery to Mount Pleasant."

"Luke, would you like to live in Charleston?"

"Oh, maybe, but that's in the future. First, I need an education."

"When we were at Cooper Hill, did you talk to Uncle Franklin about the Citadel?"

"I did, but I prefer the College of Charleston."

"That's for girls, you ninny, not boys."

"So you understand the attraction."

She slapped him on the shoulder. "You're a bad boyfriend." At her choice of words, Tessa returned to her side of the front seat.

Luke stopped the car and killed the lights. "I'm your boyfriend?" he asked.

"It just kind of slipped out." Tessa looked around. She could see nothing but a white line of breaking surf. "I guess I'd rather be out here with someone I consider a good friend instead of just any ole boy."

Luke nodded. "Got ya."

He opened the door and went around to Tessa's side. He gave her a hand getting out, then opened the back door and took out the blanket and the picnic basket. The blanket he handed to Tessa, then he shut the door. Both of them walked past the hood, stood there, and looked around, now hand in hand. They walked through the line of palmettos, crossed a low dune, and down to the water. Luke put down the picnic basket, took the blanket, and shook it out.

Tessa dropped the towels on the blanket and simply stood there. Forgotten was the flashlight.

The surf tumbled in—the tide was rising—and there were no bugs as the breeze was off the ocean. Away from the city the stars were as bright as back home in Wisconsin.

Back home, thought Luke, he and his friends would already be racing for the surf, that is, if they had a surf in Dairyland. Shouts of "last one in is a rotten egg!" would be heard up and down the beach, that is, if they had a beach.

"Well," asked Luke, "how do we do this?"

"I kind of hoped you'd turn your back and let me slip out of my clothing. Then you could join me in the water. I wouldn't look." Tessa could hear the trembling in her voice.

"Sure." Luke quickly returned to the berm and turned away from the surf.

"And no peeking."

"No, no, I'd never do that!" Luke resolutely stood with his back to the blanket.

Moments later, Tessa hollered, "Okay-dokey."

Luke turned around to see a white form splashing into the surf, and while hurrying back to the blanket, he peeled off his shirt and dropped it on the blanket. When he did, he saw something he had never really considered until this very moment. A pair of panties and a bra lay on top of Tessa's dress. He recognized them from long hours of ogling the Sears, Roebuck catalog.

Luke looked again at the surf. Was this really happening?

"Hey," shouted Tessa, from water up to her neck, "don't chicken out on me."

He didn't, and soon they were horsing around in the water, that is, until the first of the cars arrived. And if that wasn't enough, a line of boats was headed in their direction.

Rumrunners.

TWENTY-ONE

While Tessa and Luke were frolicking at the beach, Georgiana was drinking sherry in the upstairs parlor of the Belle mansion. No servants were in attendance and both doors to the parlor were closed. There was a knock at the door, and when Georgiana did not answer, the door opened and her husband, wearing his robe, walked in.

"You weren't in your bed." Though the two of them didn't sleep together—the man was a terrible snorer—Franklin always came in and kissed his wife good night.

But this time, when he came over to her chair and leaned down, Georgiana tilted her head away.

He straightened up. "What's wrong?"

She looked up at him. "You don't want to hear it."

"Of course, I do."

Georgiana finished her sherry, then handed the glass to him. "Whiskey, neat, and a larger glass!"

Franklin regarded her. "Are you sure?"

"If you're going to listen, you'll need a drink."

Franklin went over to the dry bar and poured two fingers of whiskey into his wife's glass. He returned and took the other chair. He sipped the whiskey and waited.

After a long sigh, Georgiana said, "Franklin, you have gotten this family into a fine pickle."

"What do you mean?"

"While you and your fellow club members puff away on your cigars and swap old stories, your daughter's running rings around you."

"Well," said Franklin, putting down the whiskey glass, "I certainly hope my wife isn't party to that."

"I have remained steadfastly neutral."

"That isn't very reassuring."

"You disinherit our only daughter, and when she returns to Charleston, you effectively bar her from this house."

"That's not so. Just the other night, you had Rachel and her husband over for dinner."

"Rachel and Christian as well as Nell and Franklin, but the one person who could put the stamp of approval on both relationships was not here. Did you know that Rachel has her husband looking for a house with what she calls an in-law suite?"

"What does that have to do with me? Certainly a room such as that is meant for Christian's people when they visit."

"No, my dear, I believe it's meant for me."

He drew back. "You wouldn't dare."

"My dear, you seem to forget that I'm barren and these may be the only grandchildren I shall ever have."

"But now that Franklin's to be engaged . . ."

His wife gave him the evil eye.

Clearing his throat, he added, "When we married we agreed that your being barren was not an issue."

"Because you already had children."

"And you've done a fine job of raising them."

"But will you still think so after this Sunday?"

"What's so special about this Sunday?"

"It's Rachel's intention to attend Saint Michael's with the Stuarts. Furthermore, Rachel plans to have the twins baptized Episcopalian."

"That's outrageous!"

"You thought when Rachel went north, that put an end to this, but, being a man, you forgot that a daughter always returns home to have her babies. Girls need their mothers at such a time."

Senior eyed her. "Not their fathers?"

"Franklin, dear, when are you going to learn that mothers are indispensable, fathers not so much?"

"Are you saying . . . are you saying that if I died"—he straightened up in his seat—"let me get this straight, Jeb Stuart recently passed—"

"And though his widow has spent some lonely nights, everyone in the family is far happier than they've been in years."

"How preposterous! You can't dismiss the man of the house. Who would provide for you?"

"Your successor."

"You'd remarry?" Now Franklin needed a drink. He picked up the whiskey glass and took more than a sip.

"I'm not privy to our financial arrangements so I can't say, but Mrs. Jeb Stuart will have suitors lining up at the door. She is a very rich widow."

"This is the most outlandish thing I've ever heard."

"No, my dear, it's the most outlandish thing *you've ever had to learn.*"

She reached over and took the whiskey. After a sip and a shiver, she placed it on the table. "Since I was from Georgetown, I had to work overtime to be accepted by the ladies of Charleston. What I won't do is to be a party to the humiliation of the only daughter I will ever have, the only grandchildren I may ever have."

Her husband leaned toward her. "Just tell me which woman was rude to you and I'll be happy to call on her husband."

"You see them everyday at your club."

Senior straightened up again. "I knew nothing of this, but I can sincerely say I'm willing to redress any wrong."

"How? By dueling? By fisticuffs. Aren't you a bit old for that? The only reason I had any chance of marrying you was that you already had children; otherwise you would've taken a younger bride to have your progeny."

Senior laughed. "Me take a younger bride? I hardly think so."

"Franklin, please. I'm only here because your sister made you see the sense of marrying someone your own age who could raise your children, not some young girl who would've made a fool of you and possibly the Belle name."

"I'm sorry, my dear," he said, smiling, "but I do believe I had some say in the matter."

Georgiana sighed. "Ah, yes, the vanity of men. Franklin, do you know what women call the Battery bathed in moonlight?"

Senior remembered that he had proposed to

Georgiana there, his first wife, too. "Er—no. Can't say that I do."

"A moonlit Battery is considered a woman's business office."

* * *

Christian was called to the phone on the second floor landing of James and Hartleigh's house to learn that his younger brother was in the hospital after being hit with a load of buckshot. Christian couldn't understand what his brother could've been doing to cause him to take a round of buckshot in the butt.

Eddie Elliott explained. "We've got his friend at my place. Send Stuart to fetch her."

"What?" *Her?*

But the line was dead.

Christian returned to the bedroom and told Rachel that he had to run down to the warehouse to check on a delivery.

"I thought you'd cleaned out that place."

When her husband's only reply was to pull on his coat, she forced a smile. "Well, come home soon." Rachel was not smiling when he left.

Christian found his brother at Roper where the boy lay facedown on a bed. "What's his condition?" he asked a doctor who was accompanied by a nurse holding a clipboard.

"Your brother was lucky for a boy not wearing any clothing."

"Not wearing any clothes was lucky? Why's that?"

"No, Mister Andersen. He's lucky that he wasn't killed by the buckshot because he wore no clothing."

"I don't understand."

"He was swimming off Isle of Palms."

Being one of the builders of the Cooper River Bridge, this did not comfort Christian. He understood tidal currents and riptides better than most. If anything, it made him angry that Luke would do something that stupid.

"Anyone else there?"

"If there was," said the nurse, "I hope it wasn't a girl."

Christian glared at his brother, then hustled out of the room and down the hallway to a pay phone.

As he went down the hall, the nurse called after him. "Your brother's car is parked on the street."

He turned and stared at the nurse. *Luke's car?*

She tapped her clipboard. "Says right here on the admission sheet."

And that's just where Christian found the Stuarts' Cadillac. A quick look-see located the ignition key above the visor and an empty picnic basket in the backseat along with two towels and a blanket soiled with sand.

"Who?" he asked out loud.

Tessa Stuart, of course.

Christian returned to the pay phone and called the warehouse. "Where's James?"

"Out back," said Prescott.

"Get him!"

When James came on the line, Christian updated him. "He wouldn't have been hurt so badly if he'd been wearing clothing."

"Uh-huh. They were swimming."

"And picnicking. There's a basket in the backseat of the car."

"I'm sending Alexander home. He'll drop off Prescott at Mother's. Now, give me that number and stand by that phone. I'll get right back to you."

James hung up, told Roddey who he wanted in the office, then called Eddie Elliott. "What do you want?" asked James.

"You for her."

"What's the proof?"

At the other end of the line, the phone was handed to Tessa. "Uncle James, please . . . please come get me!" She was sobbing before she finished the sentence.

In his chair behind the desk, Prescott Mitchell clinched his fists. Being from Atlanta, Prescott knew that Tessa was ruined whether she had been deflowered or not.

"Where were you and Luke tonight?"

"What?" She stopped crying. "The Isle of Palms, Uncle James, but we weren't trespassing."

"That's enough of that," said Eddie, jerking away the phone. "When will you be here?"

"Less than an hour. First, I have to check on the boy."

"I thought you'd be more worried about your niece."

"I am, but first I'm going by Roper to see how large a hammer I'm about to drop on you."

Eddie hung up and turned to his bodyguards. "They're coming. We've got less than an hour to get ready."

Tessa burst into tears, and when she wouldn't stop crying, Eddie grabbed her by the hair and forced her face up to him.

"Stop that right now!"

Tessa was immediately reduced to sniffling.

He released her hair. "You stay up here, and when the shooting starts, get in the bathtub and lie down."

Tessa glanced at the bathroom door. She'd already been in there. Twice. Once to throw up. "Yes . . . yes, sir." Tears continued down her cheeks.

Eddie gave her his handkerchief. "Take a couple of cushions, not to lie on but cover up with when the bullets start flying."

Eddie left the office, locking the door behind him. He went down the stairs, and before he reached the ground floor he was peppered with questions, the most-often asked, "We're going to war with the Stuarts?"

"There's not going to be any war. We hold the trump card."

Some of his men weren't so sure. They glanced at each other.

"What are you worried about? All you have to do is block both entrances and post guards at the doors and on the roof. When Stuart arrives, he'll do what I tell him."

One of the men wasn't convinced. "I don't know about this. This is James Stuart we're talking about."

"Hey," said Eddie, "it's a chance to twist the tiger's tail."

"And why would we want to do that?"

"Listen, you want out—go! I don't need anyone with yellow stripes backing me up."

But, of course, since they were all Charlestonians, no one backed down. Instead, they locked and loaded.

At the warehouse, James called Polly and asked her to quietly check on Tessa.

In a few minutes, Polly returned to the phone, breathless. "She's not there, and I peeked in your mother's room. Tessa's not upstairs or in the kitchen or out on the porch."

One thing you could say about Polly: she was thorough.

"Prescott's on his way home. Lock the doors and sit at the base of the stairs with the phone."

"James, where's Tessa?"

"I'm bringing her home in about an hour. She may be hysterical. Have Doctor Rose there."

"But where is she?"

But James had hung up. At Mimi's, his brother's favorite bordello, he got Jeb on the line. "Do you know who brings in the hooch for Eddie Elliott?"

"I know the little twits. The Bradshaw brothers. O'Hara went missing last year and they didn't lift a finger to find him."

"Do you know where the Bradshaws moor their boats?"

"I do."

"Sink them!"

James put his finger on the bar of the phone. He turned to Roddey, who had returned with Alexander. "Send in those two cousins of yours who think they're so tough."

"Yes, sir."

Roddey gone, James brought Alexander up to date. "Go home and lock the doors. Have Pearl and Molly take the children upstairs. Get a shotgun out of the cabinet and dig in on the second floor, but whatever you do, don't wake Hartleigh or Rachel."

"You think they're coming to the house?"

"Not at all, but when I make my play, I want

to know our families are safe." To the man in the wheelchair, he said, "Prescott, you're detailed at home. Do you have a weapon?"

Prescott nodded in the affirmative, and Alexander left the building, pushing Prescott's wheelchair ahead of him.

James called Christian and updated him. By now, people had gathered in the office, even the cops on patrol.

Into the phone, James asked, "What did Tessa mean that she and Luke weren't trespassing on the Isle of Palms?"

"I don't know. Is that important?"

"Think!"

After a long pause, Christian blurted out. "The property I bought. Tessa and Luke must've gone there for their picnic. Luke was with me when I checked it out."

Christian continued to talk, but James held the phone away from his ear. He had to think.

When he came back on the line, he said, "This is what I want you to do."

Once he finished instructing Christian, he called Lewis. "Get a judge to issue an arrest warrant for Eddie Elliott. Christian will meet you there. No, not the chief of police. This happened in the county. The sheriff."

Roddey returned with his cousins. Both men now regarded James differently since they'd heard of his run-in with Eddie Elliott.

"Do you know Elliott's trucks?"

"We do."

"Do you know where he houses them?"

They nodded.

"Burn them!"

"Yes, sir!"

"Yes, sir!"

And without a glance at their cousin, the two men left the office.

James called the chief of police. "I need an escort—lieutenant or higher."

"What about me?"

"Thank you, Chief. That's very gracious of you. Meet me at Eddie Elliott's house on Tradd Street."

"Ten minutes."

When James hung up, Roddey asked, "What do I do?"

"Man this phone, and put both patrolmen outside watching the building. You're to defend this place with your life."

Fifty-eight minutes after James had initially spoken with Eddie Elliott, he pulled up in front of the speakeasy on Market Street. James stepped out of his Buick, took off his jacket, and tossed it back in the car, revealing he wore no gun. Market Street was down to a few revelers, some passed out, and couples that wished this night would never end. Cops moved among them, encouraging them to head on home.

A plainclothes detective pulled up in a Chevy and parked beside James's Buick. "I have the warrant."

The two of them, accompanied by one of the beat cops, walked across the street where the sheriff's deputy knocked on the door.

Inside the speak, Eddie was on the phone with his wife. "Eddie, please release the girl."

"What in the world are you talking about?"

"Tessa Stuart."

"How did you know about her?"

"The Stuarts have lots of friends."

The next voice on the line was the chief of police. "Nobody has to get hurt, Eddie. Send the girl out."

"What are you doing in my house?"

"There's nothing to worry about. I have the house surrounded. Nobody's getting in or going out."

"You get the hell out of my house!"

One of the bodyguards came down the hallway from the Market Street door. "There's a deputy at the door. He has a warrant for you and all the John Does in this building."

Several of the men looked at each other. Another telephone line rang and one of the bodyguards picked it up.

"What's the charge?" demanded Eddie of the bodyguard who had come in from the front.

"Trespassing."

Eddie laughed. Into the phone, he said, "You've got to do better than that, Chief." And he hung up.

The bodyguard who had answered the other line said, "It's the Bradshaw brothers."

"What's their problem?"

"Their boats have been sunk."

There was an explosion, then a second one behind the building. Out came the pistols, even a tommy gun. A bodyguard ran in from the rear of the building, and they almost shot him.

"Hey!" he shouted, waving his arms around. "Watch it! Watch it!"

"What's the problem?"

"They've just torched the trucks."

The telephone rang. Again it was the police chief.

* * *

Hartleigh woke up when she heard voices outside her door. When her husband tried to slip into the room, she asked, "My gosh, darling, what time is it?"

"Just past one."

"Oh, James, why so late?"

"Long day at the office."

TWENTY-TWO

First, Polly had to calm Tessa, and it took several doses of laudanum to finally get her to sleep. Prescott fell asleep in his wheelchair, pistol in his lap and sitting at the bottom of the stairs. Polly finally nodded off and slept above the covers in Tessa's bed. Eileen Stuart, practically hysterical, was also given a dose of laudanum.

When Polly woke the following morning, she found Tessa and Eileen sleeping like babies, and the help anxiously gathered in the kitchen. Polly was in a quandary. Sue Ellen and Katie Stuart were out of town, Hartleigh and Rachel bedridden—what to do? In desperation she called Georgiana Belle who came right over.

Georgiana's first question was: "You say the girl's intact?"

"Yes, yes. Doctor Rose said he'd swear in a court of law."

"Well, that's the last thing we need." Georgiana

saw Prescott asleep in his wheelchair, pistol in his lap. "Don't you think your husband would be more comfortable in his own bed?"

"Oh, yes." Polly headed for the parlor.

"You might want to take his pistol away before you wake him."

She glanced back at Georgiana and lowered her voice. "Oh, yes, ma'am. I certainly will."

Polly placed the pistol on a hallway table, then rolled Prescott into their bedroom off the downstairs hallway. Prescott did not wake up until his wife helped him into bed.

"Night," said her husband, sleepily.

When Polly returned to the parlor, she found the revolver unloaded and the action broken, and Georgiana upstairs in Tessa's room.

Georgiana lifted Tessa's arm, then the other, pulled back the covers and examined under her gown. The girl slept contently.

"I don't see any bruising."

Polly shook her head. "Not a lick and I put her to bed myself."

Georgiana patted the young woman's arm. "You're a good friend, Polly. I can see why Hartleigh chose you to stay here with James's mother and his niece."

Once they were in the hallway and the door closed, the older woman asked, "Does Jeb know?"

"Not a word. James said the people working in Eddie Elliott's speakeasy know more about this than anyone else."

"Well, we shall see what we can do about that. Have you called Ashley Hall to inform them Tessa won't be at school today?"

Hand to her mouth, Polly said, "No, no, no. I

didn't think of that." She glanced at the telephone sitting on the hallway table.

Georgiana sat down, picked up the phone, and dialed a number from memory. "Mary McBee, please. Georgiana Belle calling." A moment later, she said, "You did a grand job with the library drive. We are all very proud of you. The Belle family shall have one of the very first cards." Her tone became serious. "My call is about that rascal Jeb Stuart, whom I've had to call you about before. Oh, yes, I know Tessa was a big help with the library drive. She's turning out to be a perfect Charleston lady, and we owe it all to Ashley Hall." She paused. "I'm sure the family appreciates you and the girls attending the funeral. Anyway, Jeb took Tessa and Luke Andersen, my son-in-law's younger brother, out on his boat yesterday, and the long and short of it is that Jeb did some stupid maneuver and Luke went over the side. Yes, yes, quite horrible. Boy can't swim a lick, so Tessa went in after him.

"I know, I know, what in the world was she thinking? But the girl meant well and kept Luke's head above water until they were pulled from the water. Oh, they're both fine, though Luke scraped his back rather badly in the fall. He's at Roper. My son-in-law is with him. No, no, Rachel doesn't know. Doctor Rose has both my daughter and Hartleigh Stuart in bed, but my point is that Tessa and Luke were in the water for quite a long time before Eddie Elliott pulled them out. Yes, the Eddie Elliott from that horrible place down on Market Street. Probably who Jeb was showing off for, maybe even racing.

"That's right. Disgraceful. But what are you going to do? He's a Stuart. Still, Tessa has always conducted herself with such decorum. Well, I've got to go to the hospital and relieve my son-in-law, but now you know why Tessa isn't at school today. Please let her classmates know that she'll either be there tomorrow or receiving friends at home. And if you need another donation to insure the opening of the library, just give me a call. Be a shame to come this far and fall short. Bye, bye now."

Georgiana put down the phone and let out a long sigh. For once, her rigid posture failed her and she slumped into the chair—until she saw Eileen Stuart smiling through the cracked door of her bedroom.

"Thank you, Georgiana. Nobody does that better than you."

"Oh, don't think anything of it. That's what friends are for." She left the chair, crossed the hall, took Eileen's arm, and walked her back to her bed. "You need to rest. This has all been a bit overwhelming. Polly, dear, a little help here."

Polly rushed into the bedroom and helped Eileen Stuart out of her robe and back into her bed.

Before Georgiana left, she asked, "Then we're all agreed on the story?"

"Yes," said Eileen, nodding. "Whatever you say."

Georgiana looked at Polly.

"Oh, yes, yes, yes. I'm not going to say a word."

"Very good. Tessa has her whole life ahead of her. We can't allow her father to ruin it."

"Absolutely," said Polly.

"I'm going next door and break the news to Rachel and Hartleigh. I'll send someone up from the kitchen with your breakfast. Eat hardy, ladies. We have a long way to go."

At the hospital, Luke failed to understand why such a convoluted story was required to salvage the honor of Tessa Stuart, especially when it would be often repeated that she had rescued him from the ocean.

Turning to her son-in-law, Georgiana said, "I insist you put this boy on the first train out of Charleston."

"But he's injured, Mrs. Belle."

"Christian, this is Charleston and we already have enough slow thinkers living south of Broad, and we certainly don't need another one of our girls marrying a Yankee."

Christian bristled. "You know, Mrs. Belle, it's not easy for us Yankees to stomach some of the characters we're forced to deal with south of Broad."

"Young man, don't be impertinent. I would've thought your mother had raised you better."

Christian determined that discretion was the better part of valor and shut his mouth.

Luke suffered no such restraint. He raised his head from where he lay on his chest. "You can't talk about my mother—"

"Sonny, you do yourself no favors by opening your mouth."

"Luke, this is my mother-in-law. Show some respect."

"Thank you." Georgiana continued. "I've talked with the doctor and he says Luke can leave whenever he feels like it. All you have to do is call the house and we will—"

"We'll take a taxi."

"Christian, we're trying to halt gossip, not create it."

He understood. "Luke, if a car is sent for us at three, will you be ready?"

"I just want out of this town."

Georgiana took Christian's hands in hers. "Thank you. You are a good son-in-law." She gave him a kiss on the cheek, then at the door said to the boy lying on his chest, "Young man, I would've thought more of you if you'd inquired about the condition of Tessa Stuart."

Luke opened his mouth, saw his brother glaring at him, and said, "Thank Tessa for all she's done for me, but tell her I won't be attending the Citadel this fall."

"I'll pass that along, but most of all we hope everyone remembers what a gracious young lady Tessa Stuart has become."

What astonished Christian even more was that Franklin Belle, Senior, arrived at three to take Luke home, home being the Belle mansion on South Battery.

Christian hustled to his feet. "Mister Belle, how do you do?"

They shook hands.

"Luke, this is my father-in-law. I believe you've met his son, Franklin."

Senior nodded to the boy who sat on the edge of the bed. "Georgiana says I'm to put this boy on the four-thirty train to Columbia or to bring him home for rehabilitation." A measured smiled appeared on the old man's face. "That second option may be a pun."

Luke groaned getting to his feet. "I prefer a long train ride north, if you don't mind."

"Son," said Franklin, "I sometimes feel the very same way."

Rachel was frantic by the time Christian returned to the house. "How is he?" She looked beyond her husband, who had closed the bedroom door behind him. "Where is he?"

"You're not going to believe this, but Luke is recuperating at your house."

"Are you joking? Be serious, Christian."

"Furthermore, your father insisted we join them at church Sunday, Luke, too, if he's up to it."

Rachel was speechless.

"I want to run over to the warehouse to check on a few things, then stop by and see how Luke's settling in, okay?"

Rachel could only stare at him.

"By the way, a nursery's been set up at your mother's. The room's been painted and has a rocking chair—the whole nine yards—and two bassinettes."

It was only after her husband left that Rachel finally understood. Her mother had brought to bear the enormous prestige of the Belle name to protect Tessa Stuart's reputation. Luke, Christian, and she were simply collateral beneficiaries.

TWENTY-THREE

When Christian returned to the Belle house, he found his brother behind a dressing screen with a tailor measuring him for a new suit and shirt.

"You can borrow a pair of my cuff links," said Franklin, Senior, from a chair by the door. The older man smoked a Havana cigar, and the room was rapidly filling up with smoke.

Georgiana Belle sat across the room, a fan moving the smoke around. "I'm glad you're here, Christian. I'm trying to fit your brother for evening wear and he's resisting."

"Luke, you do what Mrs. Belle says."

Senior chuckled and puffed away on his cigar.

His wife shot him a look. "You know, I don't care for cigars in this house."

"I understand, my dear, but the cigar comes with my participation in this little charade."

"She's throwing a big party for me," said Luke, smiling brightly over the dressing screen.

"It's an engagement party for our son and Nell Ingram," corrected Georgiana Belle. "Most of the important people of Charleston will be there."

"You hear that?" asked Luke. "Folks are standing in soup lines and she's throwing a party."

"When a young couple becomes engaged, you honor them with a party. It's nothing more than that."

Luke grinned as he raised an arm for a measurement. "I suppose this fine lady throws parties all the time."

"Every other week," said Senior. "No one throws a party quite like Georgiana. In Charleston, she has no peer.

"Franklin, please, you're embarrassing me."

"Sorry, my dear, but I'm rather tired of all the drivel that falls from this young man's mouth."

Christian did not know what to say, and Luke saw this from over the screen. It was, mercifully, enough to make the boy not respond for once.

"Young man," said Franklin to Luke, "my wife can bring together the wisest or the dullest of guests and make them sparkle, but you will never understand that for you are an unruly colt begging to be broken, and that's not about to happen in Charleston. We simply don't care."

Senior gestured at his wife with his cigar. "Being a good hostess takes more than money and position, or even charm or good looks. A good hostess is able to set things into motion and to fade into the background. Georgiana's at her best when she has twelve to twenty people gathered around a table where the seating arrangements are never left to chance. There is a good deal of hot blood in Charleston, and my wife appears to be one of the few hostesses able to master it."

"Yeah, well," muttered Luke, "I'm going to be somebody some day."

"Mister Winslet," said Georgiana, "please conclude your business. I don't want the boy insulting you, too."

"If the boy offends you, my dear, I can apply my buggy whip to his backside. Hard to find a good buggy whip these days."

"He's teasing, Luke."

"Am I?" Senior looked sharply at his son-in-law. "I've done it before."

"Perhaps in the war."

"Never served, much to my regret."

"I'd rather have you, darling, than a wall full of medals."

Senior sighed. "A poor substitute, my dear, after all the sacrifices our ancestors have made."

"Captain Stuart served in the Great War," said Luke from behind the screen. "He's a real hero."

"Are you saying you prefer to be horsewhipped by a veteran, because that can certainly be arranged."

Wearily, Georgiana shook her head. "How much longer, Mister Winslet?"

"Finishing now, madam."

"Very well. Luke needs to learn how to set a table and to use the correct eating utensils."

"You hear that, Christian? Your mother-in-law's turning me into a maid."

"Only if you qualify. A maid must have a modicum of brains to set a table in this house."

"Luke," asked Christian, "must you always be so generous with your opinions?"

"Undisciplined thinking." Senior tapped ashes

into an ashtray on the floor between his feet.

Georgiana smiled. "We shall change this young man's way of thinking. I look forward to it."

"Yes," said her husband. "I'm quite sure you do."

Once Georgiana saw that Luke was picking up the basics of table setting, she left him with this warning: "You will be tested on this material upon my return."

Luke grinned wickedly. "Will there be food next time? I'm starved."

"Absolutely," said Georgiana, "but if you come up short, no dessert."

Then she and her driver were off for the Stuart and Company warehouse.

"He's expecting us?" she asked from the backseat.

"Yes, ma'am," said the Negro. "I personally went down and presented your card."

At the warehouse, James received another call from his broker. "James, stocks might be down, but they're due for a rebound. People haven't stopped inventing those new laborsaving devices your wife and mine love, three radio stations have gone on the air this year alone in South Carolina, and new gas stations are still opening all across the country. Smart people are laying the groundwork for the future. You never know where the next Henry Ford, Thomas Edison, or Charles Lindbergh will come from, but one thing savvy investors know—they'll need backers."

"Look," said James, "you've got me all wrong. I wasn't a whiz at picking stocks. I simply caught the wave, then got out before the wave broke, and

I kicked myself for getting out too early. I'm never going to sell short. I'm not smart enough to do that."

"That's what you have me for. I'll pick the stocks."

Thankfully, James observed Prescott motioning for the Belle family driver to come inside the office. "Sorry," said James, "but I've got to go."

The Negro asked James to step outside, as a warehouse was not the province of any lady. James joined Georgiana in the backseat of the Buick while the driver passed the time with Alexander, smoking a cigarette.

"I want to know everything about Tessa and the Andersen boy, Captain Stuart. And please don't leave anything out."

"Nothing much to say, ma'am. Those kids had the misfortune to go swimming at a spot on Isle of Palms where rumrunners and bootleggers meet. Luke was shot when he went back for their belongings. Tessa heard him scream and went back for Luke. Once Eddie Elliott realized who Tessa was, he called me."

"Are you at liberty to give me the details?"

James shrugged. "Nothing to tell. I went down and brought Tessa home. That's all there is to it."

Georgiana eyed him. "You must have very strong powers of persuasion."

Again James shrugged.

"And Eddie Elliott turned Tessa over to you just like that." Georgiana snapped her gloved fingers.

"I made him see that it was to his advantage."

After a long moment, Georgiana said, "But you don't have a proper ending, Captain Stuart."

"I believe we do. Tessa's home safe and sound."

"Safe, yes, but Tessa's reputation is not sound."

"Ma'am?"

And Georgiana explained the new story.

"And that's why you and your brother may spend some time with people you can't tolerate this Saturday. My son will announce his engagement to Nell Ingram two days hence."

"Barring any last-minute babies, Hartleigh and I both plan to be there."

"As will my daughter, and we certainly don't need anyone upsetting them."

"That's true," said James, smiling. "We don't want them having babies at the engagement party. That would give any bridegroom second thoughts."

The next stop was Eddie Elliott's speakeasy on Market Street.

As the driver opened the door, he said, "This place is certainly something."

Georgiana glanced up and down the street, already busy in the middle of the afternoon. "I'll do my best to avert my eyes."

"Oh, no, Miss Georgiana, I didn't mean it that way."

He hurried ahead to knock on the door. When the peephole opened, he heard the familiar refrain. "No colored."

"Georgiana Belle to see Eddie Elliott. He's expecting her."

The peephole closed, the door opened, and the Negro preceded his mistress down the hall. At the turn into the main room stood another bodyguard, where they were held up while the Negro was frisked. This gave Georgiana an opportunity to look around, and she could not believe what she saw. The place was elegant, just as James Stuart had told her.

And empty.

"Are you not open today?"

"We don't open today until you and the boss finish talking."

Her driver was left at the foot of the stairs, and Georgiana followed another thick-necked bodyguard up a set of stairs where he opened the door to a small office.

But Georgiana did not immediately go inside. From the landing, she admired the dark wood, the tapestry, and the handsome dance floor and bandstand. A sparkling, long mirror ran behind the bar. Lighting was furnished by chandeliers, and right below her, a piano player warmed up playing Cole Porter. Everyone—there were no women as far as Georgiana could see—wore a tux. It looked for all the world like an exclusive men's club.

"Mrs. Belle," said the bodyguard.

She followed the large man into an office, similarly furnished.

Eddie Elliott rose to his feet behind his desk. "Nice to make your acquaintance, Mrs. Belle. I understand you are the matriarch of the Belle family of Charleston." He gestured at the sofa. "Please have a seat."

"Thank you."

A shapely redhead came out of the bathroom. She wore the typical flapper garb, but looked a bit old for such stylish clothing.

"Am I interrupting something?" asked Georgiana.

"Oh, no, Mrs. Belle. This is my wife, Maureen."

"Nice to meet you, Mrs. Belle," said Maureen Elliott. "I've heard so much about the charitable work you've done."

"Oh," said Georgiana, with a warm smile. "That sounds like you're volunteering." The two women exchanged cards, then Georgiana looked around. "I must say that you have the most amazing taste in decor."

Maureen laughed. "This has nothing to do with me. This is all Eddie's doing."

"Really?" Georgiana studied the man behind the desk. The speakeasy owner wore a three-piece suit with a club tie. Hmm. Eddie Elliott could be any businessman you met on the streets of Charleston.

"I couldn't be more proud," added Maureen.

"Where are your people from?"

"Goose Creek."

"Our family owns property up the Cooper."

"Cooper Hill."

"You've heard of it."

"Well, the Belles of Charleston are probably as well-known as the Laurens, the Pinckneys, and the Rutledges."

From where she sat on the sofa, Georgiana reached up and took the younger woman's hands. "I know this is short notice, but could you and your husband join us Saturday night? My son will be announcing his engagement to Nell Ingram."

Maureen glanced at her husband. "Well, of course. Eddie's mother lives with us and can put the children to bed."

Georgiana smiled. "I don't want to inconvenience you. Saturday night is probably a big night in . . . your husband's business."

"Mrs. Belle, I'm pleased that you would even consider us."

"Why wouldn't I? As far as the people of Charleston

are concerned, your husband's the one who fished my son-in-law's brother and his girlfriend out of the ocean."

Maureen glanced at her husband. "I hadn't heard about that."

Still holding Maureen's hands, Georgiana pulled the younger woman down beside her on the sofa. "Please allow me to tell you what a hero your husband is to the Belles of Charleston, and especially the House of Stuart."

TWENTY-FOUR

Besides joining the Round Table for lunch, Katie Stuart spent her time in New York wandering the city with her son. Jebbie, who had never been to New York, developed a crick in his neck, especially looking up at the new Chrysler Building. One day, Nicholas Eaton accompanied them.

"Will the building you and Mister Hall are working on be taller than this new Chrysler Building?" asked Jebbie.

"We hope so," said Eaton, "but you never know with William Van Alen. He snookered everyone when he topped off the Chrysler Building with a spire that made it taller than that new building on Wall Street. The spire was secretly constructed inside the building, then the base attached at the sixty-sixth floor. The spire was added the day before Black Thursday. Took about ninety minutes." Eaton smiled. "Just about as fast as the market crashed. Kind of ironic."

"Kind of sad," said Katie, looking down the street. "Nick, who are these men selling apples? I don't believe I've seen that down south."

"The apple growers of Washington State shipped them in to test the market."

"Test the market?" asked Jebbie.

"That's advertising lingo. It means to see if men can make a go of selling apples instead of going on relief. Governor Roosevelt is enthusiastic about the project. The apples only cost a nickel."

The three of them walked down the street where they quickly learned this particular businessman sold his apples for a half dollar.

"I'm grossing over sixteen dollars a day. People seem to want to help me make it through this run of bad weather until I get back on my feet."

"Well," commented Nick, "that should keep the wolf from the door."

The businessman glanced up and down the street. "Until every corner has its own apple salesman."

As they strolled away with Jebbie happily chomping on his apple, Katie asked, "Is Al Smith going to run for president again?"

"Of course."

"He got beaten pretty badly in 'twenty-eight."

"Al went through the ringer about being a Catholic and the corruption of Tammany Hall, but people don't care about that. They just want their liquor back, and they know Al's a Wet."

"For that, they'd have to pass an amendment."

"Look, I was born and raised near Boston, but I spent the last two years in Charleston building the bridge. Now I live in New York City, and I've spent a lot of weekends in Washington, DC, or Philadelphia, both just down the road. Who could be better informed as to what drinking people want? They may not get the hard stuff back, but some accommodation must be made for beer."

"Then you don't buy into the argument that drinking causes poverty, sickness, and a general loosening of moral standards?"

He grinned at Katie. "We never should've given you gals the vote. You moralize too much."

"And just what does this have to do with Al Smith?"

"Al Smith brought more new people to the polls than ever before, and they don't vote like they did down on the farm or back in the Old Country. All those new voters will insist on a candidate who'll help them get their beer back. The person who can rally them will win the presidency."

"So it's Al Smith again?"

Nick gestured at the businessman selling apples. "Unless that guy is joined by an apple seller on every corner, then it won't matter whether it's Al Smith or Franklin Roosevelt. The Republicans will be out on their butts."

Jebbie laughed, but Katie didn't crack a smile, and not because of Nick's language. James Stuart had often said that the Eighteenth Amendment would have to be repealed. Katie had called it wishful thinking, but Nicholas Eaton had lived up and down the East Coast, and as a reporter she had to give credence to that.

When they returned to the Algonquin, Sue Ellen said through a cracked bedroom door that she and Edmund would order dinner from room service.

Hearing this exchange, Jebbie said, "They sure stay in their room at lot."

Eaton laughed.

Katie explained. "I think they're down with a bug."

"Bedbugs, you call them?" said Nick, still grinning. "Let's go downstairs for the cocktail hour."

"Is that okay with you, Jebbie?"

"Sure. I love room service. And the radio. They have lots of stations in New York."

In the elevator, Nicholas said, "Would Jebbie mind if I took you to a club?"

"Just what did you have in mind?"

"A new place east of Fifth Avenue. It's called the Stork Club. Your buddy from the Round Table, Heywood Broun, discovered it quite by accident. He thought it was a funeral home."

"Doesn't sound very promising."

"Oh, hon, it's the place to be. The Stork Club has booze, jazz, and all kinds of celebrities, showgirls, movie stars, rich folks, and even the occasional count or countess."

The elevator door opened, and they stepped out.

"One trip and you may never return home." Nick escorted her to a house phone. "Call the boy and say you'll be in late tonight and to tuck himself in."

Katie gave him the evil eye.

"Oh, it's nothing like that. It's just that us lowly engineers have to wait in line to get into the Stork Club."

Turned out Nick was wrong. While they were waiting behind the rope, Ruth Hale and her husband, Heywood Broun, climbed out of a taxi and spotted them standing in line.

"Lady Lindy!" shouted Ruth. "Do come inside with us."

They did, and Katie Stuart was put on the list by Sherman Billingsley, a former bootlegger from Oklahoma who had heard of the House of Stuart.

"You're welcome anytime, Mrs. Stuart. Your family and mine are in the same business, and we have to look out for each other."

As they made their way across the crowded floor, Nick leaned over and said, "Now it's me that never wants you to return to Greenville."

A visit to New York is not complete without a carriage ride through Central Park, so the following day Katie, Jebbie, and Nick hired a horse-drawn cab, only to find that Central Park had changed. The park was now occupied by the homeless, the indigent, and the usual hobos.

"Stop the carriage!"

Katie stood up. She had never seen such a huge shantytown. Sure, similar groups occupied the banks of the Reedy River where it cut through Greenville; families had even taken up living under bridges and railroad trestles, but here, a small town had grown up in Central Park—home to some five hundred people and more shacks going up everyday.

Policemen patrolled the camp but none of the inhabitants appeared particularly threatening. A line of women and children stretched through the camp, each with a bucket or empty can. In one spot, men pulled down a series of structures that had burned during the night, and many of them yelped when the salvaged piece they coveted was found to still be hot. Metal smokestacks, cast iron grates and grills and pots and pans were all that was left after the fire.

"What is this place?" asked Katie, tightening her grip on Jebbie's shoulder.

"This is where people come when they have no one to take them in. It's called Hooverville," said Nick.

"Named for the president?"

"Actually, the Democrats gave these towns that name, and the poor souls share food like communists. When their commissary gets low, they send out men to see what the hotels are throwing away."

"They're eating garbage?"

"They are."

"The children, too?"

Nick nodded.

"That's appalling." In the past, only hobos dug through your garbage or stole cooling pies from your kitchen windowsill.

"A whole culture has sprung up. Newspapers are called 'Hoover blankets,' cardboard worn inside a shoe with holes in the soles is called 'Hoover leather,' and 'Hoover hankies' are when you pull your pocket inside out, revealing that you have no money."

Katie remembered the foreclosed farm in Florence County. A jackrabbit had been startled out of a bush and the farmers had laughed at their misfortune. Their rifles were in their trucks. One of the farmers had called the jackrabbit a "Hoover hog." Everyone had laughed.

But no one was laughing here.

Katie made a complete turn, scanning the area. "But where did all these squatters come from?"

"New York, or hereabouts."

Katie stared at him. "They're locals?"

"Who couldn't pay the mortgage or lost their lease."

"But this place is huge. It dominates the Great Lawn."

People were living in wooden shacks, boxes, or pup tents, along with the occasional well-built wooden or stone structure. Evidently stonemasons and carpenters had been thrown out of work, too. Adults just sat there, glum looks on their faces. Small children stared blankly from piles of trash. People with no hope.

"Are we going?" asked the driver. "I've got a living to make."

Katie hopped down from the carriage, quickly followed by her son. "Pay the man, Nick."

Out of her clutch purse came her steno pad and she began making notes. "Stay close, Jebbie."

Nick joined them as the driver slapped the reins and the carriage drove off.

"Ever the reporter," he said, smiling.

"We don't have this back in Carolina."

"Or perhaps you've never gone looking for it."

A man strode through the camp with a piece of plywood under one arm and several two-by-fours under the other. Hooked to his belt was a hammer. Piles of trash burned on the Great Lawn, also in 55-gallon drums. When Katie peered inside one of the structures, she saw a small stove, backseats from automobiles being used for beds, and simple cooking implements. Maybe there was extra clothing in the shelter's darkness, but Katie never saw it.

"Here live the most resourceful pack rats in the city," said Nick.

"But why doesn't someone do something about it?"

"Governor Roosevelt's trying, but there's so much graft that the relief rarely makes it down to this level."

Jebbie had wandered over to a group of boys and now was down on his knees shooting marbles in the dirt. Jebbie always carried at least one marble at all times.

"That's a cat's-eye, man!" shouted one of the boys. "It's the only one I've got."

"Hey, I won it fair and square!"

Katie tried to call Jebbie, but her voice failed her. Tears ran down her cheeks. She wiped them away. A car passed by—pulled by a team of horses.

Nicholas put his arm around her. "You're not in Carolina anymore."

Katie sobbed into his shoulder. "And worlds away from the Stork Club."

* * *

Back in Charleston, an imperious Rachel Belle dared her twins to ruin her brother's special evening. Her water had broken during one of her many trips to the bathroom.

Rachel had done everything the doctor had asked, but she'd be darned if she'd miss her brother's engagement party.

She listened impatiently to Katie's travelogue, then asked, "How did Nick look?"

"Exceptionally dapper."

"Then I'd rather him not see me in my condition."

In Hartleigh's room she heard the first inquiry regarding Sue Ellen.

"You know," said Katie, "I think she's finally content."

"I never thought I'd hear that word used to describe my sister-in-law. Hope I get a letter soon."

Katie laughed for the last time that evening. "It may take a while. She and Edmund were still catching up when I left."

"How did you find New York?"

Hoovertown flashed through Katie's head. "Let's just say it wasn't entirely like I remembered."

In the house next door, Jeb, Junior, asked James, "Why are you telling me all this rigmarole about Tessa being rescued by Eddie Elliott? It was nothing like that."

"Because Elliott and his wife will be here tonight."

"Seriously? The Belles are entertaining that low-life? Why?"

"Mother can't do it, so the Belles are honoring Elliott for saving Tessa and Luke's lives."

"But you and I did that, plus the chief of police. By the way, did you bonus him?"

"An extra fifty."

"For making a phone call."

"He'll be there tonight, Jeb."

"Good. We'll need someone to break up the fights."

"There will be no fights."

Jeb grinned. "Really?"

"You start a fight and you seal your daughter's fate. She'll be cast out of Charleston society, and no telling who she'll end up marrying, but it'll be whoever will condescend to have her."

"Tessa's better than that."

"But only if her father doesn't pick a fight tonight."

TWENTY-FIVE

The line through the reception area of the Belle mansion was long and trailed out on the porch. Local, state, and national officeholders, and former local, state, and national officeholders, including a former governor who had regularly bashed Charleston as the "Sodom and Gomorrah" of the Carolinas, were all in attendance.

Knowing he would find James at this event, his broker sought him out, even before James and Hartleigh went through the front door. When they arrived—fashionably late—the broker drew James aside on the front porch.

"Is there a place for me in your organization? With the market down, none of my clients are buying stocks, and I'm ashamed to be seen at my Rotary club."

"See me at the warehouse tomorrow morning and we'll see what we can do."

At the head of the receiving line stood the engaged

couple flanked by Franklin and Georgiana as the hosts; on the other side were the Ingrams and two of their adult children, both of whom were married. Christian was next in line with Rachel seated beside him. And both Rachel and Christian overheard more than once:

"Guess the silly rumors were wrong about the disinheritance."

"Well, anyone can put on a happy face."

Across the hall in the parlor, Tessa Stuart was surrounded by her classmates, and members of the Pinckney and Laurens families commented on the girl with the tanned face and bright smile.

"Girl looks fine."

"I would've put her in line with Nell and Franklin."

"It's not her day," cautioned 'Pink' Pinckney. "It's Nell's."

"Clever of Georgiana to present this as just another engagement party. Why, Eileen Stuart isn't even here."

"Ah, yes, they are playing this by the book."

"Oh, look who's coming through the line. It's James with Katie on his arm, and his brother, Jeb, with Hartleigh on his arm. Well, now, that is one pregnant young lady."

"And I thought it was Rachel who was expecting twins." Looking around, Pink asked, "Where's Sue Ellen?"

"In New York with her husband, I heard."

"As she should be. That girl was a scandal just waiting to happen."

"And who comes through the door right behind the Stuarts but Billy Ray and Grace Craven."

"They say Billy Ray's to run for solicitor."

Dottie sneered. "Well, it takes a thief . . ."

"I don't see how Grace stays with him."

"Oh, Pink, Grace knows all about Billy Ray's dalliances. She hopes to one day sleep in the governor's mansion."

"That may not be enough. Charleston ladies forgive but they never forget."

"Oh, my, look! It's that speakeasy owner, Eddie Elliott."

"Well, I declare! Guess it's true that Elliott did pull those poor children from the ocean."

Luke Andersen walked through the door, tentatively.

Pink saw him first. "And a bigger sourpuss than Luke Andersen couldn't be found."

"How he can stand being in a town where it's known that a girl saved him from drowning, I don't know."

But Dottie was staring at Rachel Andersen bent over in her chair in the receiving line. "If I didn't know better, I'd swear that girl's having contractions."

Once through the line, Katie was escorted into the dining room where the long table had its chairs removed and was covered with finger food. Every light in the house had been turned on, supplemented by candles. Black servants passed through the crowd with trays of champagne.

It was here that Katie's nerve finally broke when she overheard Luke Andersen say, "What a spread! I ought to take some of this down to the soup kitchen."

Katie burst into tears and raced from the room.

Startled, Hartleigh asked, "What did you say?"

James was befuddled. "Nothing, dear. I swear,

nothing at all."

"Don't swear, James." And Hartleigh followed Katie out of the dining room.

"What the devil was that all about?" asked Jeb.

"I have no idea. If you ask me, women become even more screwy when they get pregnant."

Hartleigh found Katie on the back porch, sobbing into a handkerchief.

"Katie, dear, are you all right?"

"No! No! Never!"

"I don't understand."

"That boy's right. Nothing's right about this."

"What boy?"

"Luke Andersen."

"Now, if my brother-in-law's been rude, please to be patient with him. He'd never been south of the Mason-Dixon Line before he came to Charleston."

"No, no. Not that." Katie dabbed at her eyes. "I shouldn't tell an expectant mother this, but I've seen the future and it's absolutely horrid. The rich get richer and the poor starve to death."

A pretty redhead who would graduate from Ashley Hall in a few weeks approached Luke in the dining room. "Aren't you the boy Tessa saved from drowning?"

Instantly, Luke's face clouded up. "It wasn't that way at all. What happened was . . ."

Luke saw Molly, Alexander's sister-in-law, staring at him from across the room. As was James Stuart once his wife left to follow Katie.

"Er . . . nothing," bit off Luke. He left the room.

James stopped him in the hallway. "Did you

excuse yourself?"

"For what?"

"You must ask permission to leave a young lady's presence."

"The devil I do!"

"It's called polite society, and you'd do well—"

"I'm sick of polite society."

James studied the boy. "I'll personally drive you to the train station if you'll tell me what Tessa Stuart ever saw in you."

Luke looked around and saw more eyes watching, and that included his brother. He did not, however, see Tessa watching from the parlor right behind him.

"Why wait until tomorrow," sneered Luke. "I'm ready to go right now. Anyway, I'm sick of all the phonies in this town." He stormed down the hallway and out the door.

At the other end of the hallway, Eddie Elliott greeted Jeb with an out-thrust hand. "Good to see you again, Jeb. I'm pleased I could be of assistance to the Stuart family." Eddie grinned like a house afire.

Maureen Elliott did not smile. Matter of fact, Maureen didn't expect to smile all evening. There was something off-putting about being in any house on South Battery.

Jeb looked at the outstretched hand. "I've got nothing to say to you, Elliott."

But before Elliott could withdraw his hand, James came up from behind and took Eddie's hand, putting his other hand on the man's shoulder.

When Eddie tried to pull away, James said, "I want to personally thank you for all you did for the Stuart family. We are in your debt, Eddie."

At that, Maureen almost smiled.

"And, Mrs. Elliott, you are looking particularly radiant this evening."

Now she did smile. "Thank you, Captain Stuart."

James released her husband's hand and looked around. "I'd like to introduce you to my wife, but I appear to have lost her."

Jeb snorted and pushed his way through the Elliotts, down the hallway, and out the front door.

Luke had stormed outside, intent on returning to James and Hartleigh's house. There he would pack a bag and walk down to the train station. He'd be gone in the next few hours. But before Luke could remember that his suitcase was in the house he had just stormed out of, four men intercepted him at the curb.

One man put a hand on Luke's chest, stopping him. "Remember us, boy?"

Luke recognized the men from the roadblock, two of the four whom Rachel had shot.

Luke made a break to return to the house, but they grabbed him.

"Not so fast," said Magnus, holding the boy at the curb.

Kasper gestured at the house. "This where your brother lives with his bitch?"

"Rachel's no bitch!"

Kasper slapped him. "Answer the question, kid. Is this the home of Rachel and Christian Andersen?"

Jeb came down the steps two at a time. As he passed, he saw Luke Andersen being slapped.

"What's going on here?"

Kasper said, "None of your business, fella."

Magnus asked, "Are you a Belle of Charleston?"

"Hardly."

"Then move along."

Jeb looked from one man to the other. "Yankees?"

Setting his jaw, Magnus asked, "What's it to you, reb?"

"What's going on here?" Jeb asked Luke.

"Rachel shot two of these men when they tried to stop us from leaving Wisconsin." Luke pointed out Kasper and Magnus. "Plugged them both."

"Well," said Jeb with a broad grin, "as Teddy used to say: bully for her. Still, you'll have it easier this time. Rachel's so pregnant she just might pop if you look at her the wrong way."

All four men looked at the house. "What's going on? Some kind of a party?"

"Yeah," said Luke with a laugh. "While ordinary people work to keep their heads above water, the Belles of Charleston throw a party every week."

The four men looked at each other.

One said, "I don't understand."

"Push off, boys," said Jeb. "Most of the men inside that house attended the Citadel, and they were raised on the hope of someday kicking some Yankee butt."

"Well, then," said Kasper, smiling, "maybe we should warm up with you."

Another grin from Jeb and the usual retort from a member of the Stuart clan. "You can try."

Luke rushed into the house, down the hallway, and interrupted James and Hartleigh talking with the Elliotts. Hartleigh had requested a chair, and James had brought one from the study.

Luke grabbed James's arm. "Come quick. Jeb's gotten into another fight."

"Dammit! He promised not to get into any fights tonight."

James apologized for his language, then placed his champagne glass on a table and followed the boy down the crowded hallway. At that same moment, Hartleigh's water broke.

"James! Please don't leave me!"

James looked at his wife, her face white with fear. He glanced at the front door and decided that for once, his brother was on his own.

"You take care of your wife," said Eddie Elliott. "I'll look into this."

"Thanks."

On his way out the front door, Luke stopped at the reception room and shouted to his brother, "The two men Rachel shot are out front. You've got to get her out of here!"

And with that, Rachel gave in to the inevitable, gasping in pain when the next contraction hit.

TWENTY-SIX

It became the most calamitous engagement party ever held south of Broad. People talked about it for years, to the great distress of Georgiana Belle.

With his brother's call to action, Christian broke for the door but was called back by his wife. Not only was Rachel hit with another contraction, but she was peppered with questions.

"You actually shot someone?" asked her mother.

"What were the circumstances?" demanded her father. "Did those Yankees mistreat you while you were up north?"

Franklin and Nell and the Ingram family could only stare at the pregnant woman. Their special night had been upstaged by the wildest of rumors.

Reaching for his wife, Christian said, "We need to get Rachel home."

Georgiana put a hand on his shoulder. "She is home, Christian."

"What? Oh, right." He scooped up his wife.

"Rachel will point out her old room upstairs."

Rachel smiled. "Thank you, Mama."

As Christian carried his wife into the hallway and toward the stairs, Rachel smiled to all those gathered in the hallway. Before they went up the stairs, Rachel made Christian face the crowd.

"Once I've delivered these babies, I expect many of you to come calling, and I want to hear everyone's stories about what a gay ole time you had tonight at my brother's engage—"

Rachel was cut off by another contraction, and Christian rushed his wife upstairs as shouts, yelps, and threats of grievous bodily harm floated through the door from the front yard. Most of the men, and the cadets in dress uniforms, ushered wives into the kitchen or the study, evacuating the front of the house. But the Ashley Hall girls, well, this was too good to pass up. They headed for the front porch.

The porch could barely hold everyone, but the Ashley Hall girls had a front row seat at what would later be called The Third Battle for Charleston, the first being the seizing of the city by the British, the second, occupation by Yankees.

When Luke raced out of the house and down the steps, he had no idea that he was on his own. Seeing Jeb on the ground and being kicked by Kasper, Luke leaped on the man—and bounced off his shoulder.

"Get away from me, kid," said Kasper.

This enabled Jeb to recover enough to wrap his arms around Kasper's legs, tripping the Wisconsinite and bringing him down to his level. But Jeb had little chance to use his advantage as Magnus knocked Jeb's head into the sidewalk and Jeb went out like a light.

Regaining his feet, Kasper muttered, "Now you're not so tough."

"I am!" shouted Luke, and he slammed into Kasper again, this time driving a shoulder into the older man.

One of the other three men grabbed Luke from behind and held the boy while Kasper slapped him. After several blows, Luke slumped in the second man's arms.

"Damn kid." Kasper wiped his hands on his pants. "Now we find his brother if we have to pull down this house to do it."

So the remaining three were caught by surprise when a white tornado raced down the sidewalk and leaped on the man holding Luke from behind. Tessa rode the man's back, hanging on for dear life and tightening her grip around the man's throat.

"She's choking me." Unable to dislodge the girl or even breathe, he finally got out, "Give me some help here." It came out as a gurgle.

But the other three had opened the gate and headed up the sidewalk to the Belle mansion, leaving the fourth man to Luke, who had, once again, staggered to his feet and began to punch the man's stomach repeatedly. The girls on the porch cheered and waved their white handkerchiefs.

One incurable tomboy who felt stifled by being raised as a lady turned to her friend. "I don't know about you, but that looks like too much fun to pass up." And she rushed down the steps.

When Tessa went flying off the man's back, the tomboy leaped aboard. Quickly, several girls were down the steps and picking up Tessa. The tomboy was twirled around as the fourth man had to deal with a pesky Luke Andersen, who wouldn't stop throwing punches at his midriff.

The Wisconsinite had had enough. He drew back to knock Luke into next week when the tomboy took a bite out of his ear. The man screamed, and this caused Jeb to regain consciousness and, being the veteran of many a bar fight, lifted his opponent's trousers and bit the man on the ankle.

Again, the Wisconsinite screamed, and then, while he was off-balance, Luke delivered a final blow that caused the man to stumble into the cobblestone street where he sat there dazed as several girls from Ashley Hall pummeled him with their delicate little fists.

Luke backed off, legs wobbly, vision blurred, and then he, too, sat down and fell back on the sidewalk.

Tessa knelt beside him, picked up his head, and placed it in her lap. She kissed his cheek. "My hero!"

Luke smiled up at her. "That sounds a lot better than what I've been hearing lately." He drew her down and kissed her, then lost consciousness.

Kasper, Magnus, and the third member of their party, Tobias, marched up the front steps where they ran into Franklin Belle, Eddie Elliott, and Billy Ray Craven.

"I'm assistant solicitor for Charleston County," said Billy Ray. "What's your business here in Charleston?"

"We're looking for Christian Andersen."

"My brother-in-law," said Franklin.

"That'll do for a start." Kasper delivered a punch that connected with Franklin's jaw, which all his friends knew was made of glass and why Franklin carried a cane. Franklin crumpled to the porch. Nell, watching through the window, shrieked.

"Yankees?" inquired Billy Ray.

"Why's that so important to you people?" Kasper swung at Billy Ray, who dodged the blow and righted himself.

"You'll have to do better than that, Yankee boy."

"I can," said Kasper, setting up a roundhouse blow.

But before he could deliver, Billy Ray stepped in close and knocked the wind out of Kasper and sent him stumbling back down the stairs.

Magnus took this chance to pop Billy Ray, which knocked the solicitor into a group of Ashley Hall girls. They shrieked in surprise. My goodness, thought the girls, this was more fun than a petting party.

Tobias took a poke at Eddie Elliott, but a fist was already headed his way. Eddie knocked Tobias back, so that he, too, had to retrace his steps down the steps.

And because the blood of the warrior class flowed through these Charlestonians, they foolishly left the high ground and descended the steps.

Inside the house, Rachel had been assisted into her former bedroom while Hartleigh lay in a twin-bed guest room across the hall. Both women had had their dresses and undergarments removed and nightgowns slipped over their heads. This was enough to scatter James and Christian even before the unladylike remarks began.

"Why don't you go knock the fool out of one of those boys from Wisconsin?" demanded an angry Rachel Andersen from her bed. The rest of the insult was lost in another scream.

Heading downstairs, Christian caught up with James, who had been thrown out of his delivery room, much to his relief. "I don't think my wife will ever forgive me."

"Well, it does explain why married men complain of a severe lack of relations with their brides."

On the porch, they found Franklin Belle being treated with a towel full of ice by his fiancée; Christian's brother being tended to by Tessa Stuart near the sidewalk; and a Wisconsinite writhing in the street and holding his bleeding leg.

Eddie Elliott and Billy Ray were duking it out with Magnus and Tobias, and Jeb had passed out, a smile on his face. When Billy Ray went down, several Citadel cadets thought they could stand in for the grownups but quickly learned that Wisconsin farmers were more than a match for a bunch of cadets.

"I think you're looking for me!" shouted Christian as he rushed down the steps and threw a punch.

Kasper's nose exploded in blood, and James went toe to toe with Magnus, slugging it out near the gate. Everyone was holding his own until Franklin, Senior, waded into the fight with his buggy whip.

"Disrespect my daughter, will you?"

And soon the four dairy farmers were running in the general direction of the train station with the older man in hot pursuit.

The chief of police and his wife watched as the chaos spilled across South Battery.

"I told you, honey," said the chief, "when you arrive late to a party held south of Broad, you chance missing all the fireworks."

EPILOGUE

When Sue Ellen, Rachel, and Hartleigh had put together their triple wedding, literally marrying in the shadow of the first bridge built across the Cooper River, their bridegrooms created a pool as to which of the young women would produce the first child. Sue Ellen, because of the miscarriage, was disqualified, and unbeknownst to the remaining two women, other men wanted in on the bet.

Billy Ray Craven put fifty bucks on Hartleigh, then another fifty when Sue Ellen decamped for New York. Prescott Mitchell bet fifty on Hartleigh and Franklin bet fifty on his sister, then, when he glimpsed Rachel upon her return to Charleston, Franklin bet another hundred on Rachel. You could bet as much and as often as you wished, and the date and time of each bet was posted in a notebook kept by James Stuart.

Lewis Belle overheard the conversation and added fifty dollars to the pot for his niece. Alexander was in for twenty-five on Hartleigh; Jeb, Junior, for a hundred on his brother's wife. Several warehouse employees kicked in smaller amounts, including those working at what was now called the Chase Factory Warehouse, as did most of the hands on Jeb's boat. Cousin Jimmy knew of the pool but was afraid to chip in because of what Katie would think. But Franklin, Senior, hearing of the pool at his club, of all places, demanded to be allowed in for twenty-five dollars; then, when he glimpsed the size of his daughter upon her return to Charleston, he put in another fifty.

Luke Andersen learned of what he thought was a World Series pool and had James put him down for ten dollars on the St. Louis Cardinals. (The Cards lost in four games to Connie Mack's Philadelphia Phillies who repeated as world champs.)

As for the baby pool, Rachel delivered first (a boy), then waited around for the boy's twin to appear but her contractions had stopped. Astonishingly, twins were delivered across the hall by Hartleigh, who could not understand why her contractions continued well past the delivery of a daughter.

All of this information was duly reported from the top of the stairs by Luke Andersen, who had drunk a little too much champagne and was close to being blotto. When Luke reported that "Doctor Rose believes there's another baby still inside Hartleigh," side bets were made.

"Boy or girl. Place your bets! No script, no checks, only the new Yankee notes."

Exhausted from the first delivery, Hartleigh could only lie there, knowing she'd immediately have to get pregnant again because James so much wanted a son.

When the boy arrived, Hartleigh collapsed in

exhaustion, hair soaked, and the babies lying in the crooks of both arms. James beamed and passed out another round of Havanas. Molly and Pearl each snatched up a baby and paraded their new charges around the landing. And quickly the rumor spread that Rachel Andersen was in a huff because of being bested by Hartleigh.

When James learned it was feeding time, he left the birthing room to pass out more cigars, and on the landing, Senior demanded two cigars. He was immediately reprimanded by his wife.

"The old fool about killed himself chasing those Yankees out of town. You do wish to live long enough to spoil this grandchild, don't you?"

"That I do," agreed her husband.

Junior reached over and plucked the extra cigars from the front coat pocket of his father's jacket. "Then I'll keep these for the future."

Nell flushed and looked away.

Georgiana escorted Nell into the room where Rachel had finished feeding her son, Nell's soon-to-be nephew. Downstairs, they heard Christian talking long distance to his family in Dairyland.

"Yes, yes, it's a boy, and you should see his blond hair."

"Name?" inquired Georgiana, closing the door behind her.

Nell picked up the baby and cooed to it.

"Jonathan Bent Andersen," said Rachel.

"Bent?" asked Georgiana.

"Christian's uncle who encouraged him to leave the farm and to get an education. He's a circuit court judge who couldn't stand the thought of another family member wasting his life as a hardscrabble farmer. I've met the man, Mama, and I can tell you he's absolutely charming—"

"For a Yankee?" asked her stepmother with a smile.

Rachel nodded. "And I'm in total agreement, otherwise I never would've met the love of my life." She gestured at the baby in Nell's arms. "Look what Christian has given me!"

"No, my dear, look what you've given Christian. You must always keep your husband on his toes."

In the guest room, Hartleigh smiled up at her husband. "Names, James? The boy will certainly be named for you, but what about the girl? Your mother? My mother? Both?"

James took a seat on the bed and took his wife's hand. "What about 'Mary Anne'? You and your sister were twins, and now we have a pair, so why not? That is, if you don't object."

"Oh, no, I love the idea. Mary Anne Stuart it is."

"Mary Anne Randolph Stuart. Maiden names are much more important when you live south of Broad."

"Oh, James, that reminds me. Did I tell you that I received a cable from my mother? She's returning to Charleston to help me with the babies."

ABOUT THE AUTHOR

Steve Brown is the author of the Belle family saga, which begins when Catherine and Nelie Belle arrive in Charles Towne just in time for Nelie to be kidnapped by Blackbeard and carried off to the Outer Banks. One hundred fifty years later, and before the outbreak of the Civil War, the sixth generation of the Belle family owns a huge rice plantation up the Cooper River; Franklin Belle goes to West Point, his brother, Lewis, to the Citadel. Fifty years following that, three old maids, the great, great grandchildren of Catherine, take in an orphan, a victim of the moonshine feuds in the Carolina foothills. Fifteen years later, the Belle family is part of the Charleston scene during the Roaring Twenties; a year later, the effects of the Panic of 1929 hits, and during the Sixties, Ginny Belle, thirteenth generation Charlestonian, spends her summers on Pawleys Island where she and her friends go to meet boys and dance.

The Pirate & the Belle
The Belles of Charleston
The Old Maids' Club
Charleston's Lonely Heart Hotel
Charleston's House of Stuart
Carolina Girls

Bibliography

The Buildings of Charleston
Jonathan H. Poston

Charleston: A Historic Walking Tour
Mary Preston Foster

The Illustrated Encyclopedia of Costume & Fashion
Jack Cassin-Scott

The Early Architecture of Charleston
Albert Simons and Samuel Lapham, Jr.

The Forgotten Man
Amity Shlaes

The Great Depression
Robert S. McElvanie

A History of the American People
Paul Johnson

Isle of Palms
Wendy Nilsen Pollitzer

Last Call: The Rise and Fall of Prohibition
Daniel Okrent

Only Yesterday: An Informal History of the 1920's
Frederick Lewis Allen

A Patriot's History of the United States
Larry Schweikart and Michael Allen

A Short History of Charleston
Robert Rosen

Since Yesterday
Frederick Lewis Allen

South Carolina: A History
Walter Edgar

The South Carolina Encyclopedia
Edited by Walter Edgar